Gordon S. Dickson was born near Inverness, Scotland, but left there at a young age when the family returned to Northern Ireland.

He was educated at secondary and grammar schools and scraped through English 'O' level, as essay writing was not a strong point.

He was employed in the Civil Service for several years but is now retired and has only recently taken up writing novels. 'The Heir…Apparently, A Bartonshire Tale 3' is his eighth novel.
It includes a short story: Ashes to Ashes.

He enjoys reading several genres of books but mainly historical and detective novels, and gardening.

Other books by this author:
Verdict Unknown
Verdict Unknown… the Sequel
The Sheriff of River Bend
Des Pond, Special Agent
The Wartime Adventures of Harry Harris (Bartonshire Tale 1)
An Impossible Quest (A Bartonshire Tale 2)
The Life and Times of Victoria-Ann Penny (for children)

For all our Health Service workers

Gordon S. Dickson

THE HEIR…APPARENTLY, AND ASHES TO ASHES, A SHORT STORY

A Bartonshire Tale 3

AUSTIN MACAULEY PUBLISHERS™

LONDON • CAMBRIDGE • NEW YORK • SHARJAH

A CIP catalogue record for this title is available from the British Library.

ISBN 9781398424777 (Paperback)
ISBN 9781398424784 (ePub e-book)

www.austinmacauley.com

First Published 2023
Austin Macauley Publishers Ltd®
1 Canada Square
Canary Wharf
London
E14 5AA

Thanks to my cousin Esme Briggs for her assistance.

Thanks are also due to Mr George Ruddock for the initial idea of human remains found in a church (based on a real incident) for 'Ashes to Ashes'. He also reviewed the whole book with some useful comments.

Thanks also to Andrew J Millen for tips on fishing and a few puns.

The Heir... Apparently

A Bartonshire Tale 3

'Hello, my name's George Charles Frederick Rupert Beaumont-Foxwood. My parents could not decide on a name for their first-born son when I arrived, yelling blue murder, into this beautiful world in St Chad's Hospital, Kensington, London. So, I am lumbered with that lot! Just call me George and certainly not Rupert, I hate it!

'This is a short history of our family, of how we came to be living in Market Barton. It tells how… okay, you will need to read on to find out. Enjoy!

'I'm off for a cup of tea.'

Chapter 1
Things Were Difficult for
the Lawyers

The morning edition headlines (Monday, July 15, 2019.) in the "London Daily Post" newspaper read as follows:

TRAGEDY AT SEA. Breaking news: It is feared all 1,563 souls on-board were lost with the sinking of the liner Empress Victoria. Among the lost, it is feared, were the Ninth Duke and Duchess of Bartonshire and their two young sons, Gregory and Cedric Beaumont, who have been lost presumed drowned, when the ill-fated liner on which they were travelling to New York, sank in a freak storm off Land's End late yesterday.

There have been no survivors reported so far. The search is continuing while hope lasts. Coastguard helicopters and vessels are systematically covering the area our source reports. Some debris has washed up on local beaches.

A Royal National Lifeboat Institution spokesperson said: 'Due to the unexplained sudden sinking of the vessel, it is feared no one managed to launch a lifeboat. Only one partial distress call was received. Nothing else has been heard or seen since. Locals cannot recall such a fearsome storm within living memory.' There is speculation that a tsunami type wave overwhelmed the ship, though this has yet to be confirmed.

As we await further news reports Her Majesty the Queen has ordered that flags will be flown at half-mast on all public buildings. Her condolences have been sent to the families of the lost.

Plans for a national memorial service in Westminster Abbey to be held next Sunday have been mooted.

The late Duke's family lawyers, Messrs Grimm, Grimm and Grimes, of Mayfair, London, immediately set about the task of locating an heir to the title, the Duke of Bartonshire, with the aid of the "College of Arms", the "Royal College of Heraldry" and "Debrett's Peerage and Baronetage". No males were obviously in contention as many of the relatives had died, and with Gregory having been the heir apparent and Cedric the 'spare', the late duke had not bothered to bring the family tree up to date, mainly as it would have cost money. So, the lawyers resorted to expanding the known Beaumont Family Tree. It dated back to the first duke who was awarded the title, Montague Delacour George Beaumont, in the year 1760.

The First Duke had been granted the title for distinguished service to the Crown in the army, led by General James Wolfe, in the war against the old enemy, namely the French, in Canada.

George III, the newly crowned King, had also granted the First Duke twenty thousand acres in the County of Bartonshire, and ten thousand pounds *per annum* for life, an enormous sum in those days.

The Duke proceeded to build an enormous mansion as befitted, as he thought, his new status. He attended the House of Lords, though travel in those days was slow and arduous. It was speculated by some wags at the time that he was only too glad to get away from the Duchess for a few days! She was a formidable lady by all accounts. He attended the Lords often! 'They really need my input, my dear,' he told her.

Parish records of marriages and baptisms in the County of Bartonshire were dusted off and scrutinised minutely by the lawyers. No page was left unturned. The Registry of Births, Deaths and Marriages was also scrutinised.

Things were difficult for the lawyers. The First Duke had six legitimate sons, (his numerous illegitimate sons did not signify). The Second Duke had four, and so on. Most of the lines had died out, as children, even of the nobility, tended to die in infancy, but eventually, they found that the third son of the Third Duke had a living male descendant, albeit distant. They proceeded to locate this male who, they discovered to their surprise, worked in a market in South London. It was only a few minutes' drive from their offices.

After consulting a stout lady, behind a stall, selling costume jewellery, Mr Augustus Grimm senior, his son Mr Augustus Grimm junior, and Mr Oswald Grimes, a nephew, like a latter-day "three wise men" in pin-striped suits, briefcases in hand, bowler hats firmly in place, approached a rather scruffy individual in the London market one day. The man owned a fish stall, and the smell was overpowering… and that was just his body odour!

The market was held twice weekly in a square just south of the River Thames not far from Southwark. About fifty stalls with brightly coloured awnings covered the area.

Trade was good that sunny morning. Lots of shouting: 'Fresh veg! Get yer fresh veg 'ere,' 'Tayters an' carrots fresh from the groun'!' or 'Lovely fresh fish! Get yer fresh fish 'ere! None fresher, none cheaper in all merry England!'

'Excuse me, sir,' said Mr Augustus Grimm, the senior partner, doffing his hat, 'but may we have a moment of your time?' Mr Augustus Grimm senior rarely left his office as he was getting old and gout troubled him, but as it involved a potential duke, he broke the habit of decades. He should have retired years ago!

Mr Augustus Grimm senior was tall and thin but was slightly stooped with age. His hair was white and cut short and neat. He had a rather bony face with a pointed jaw, sharp nose and a trimmed moustache. Mr Grimm junior was a fac-simile of his papa, but his hair was still dark. Mr Grimes was short and plump, and his face showed many old acne scars from his youth.

The scruffy individual saw three smartly dressed geezers in pinstriped suits, bow ties, and bowler hats, and was not a little perturbed.

'I ain't done nothing, Guv'nor. I've paid me tax,' he de-clared, thinking *taxmen*. He wiped his hands on a grubby apron. The three men wisely did not offer to shake hands!

'We are not here to cause you bother, Mr Beaumont. That is your name, Charles Alexander Glen Beaumont, is it not?' asked Mr Grimes.

Beaumont nodded hesitantly. 'Erm, yeah, that it is. What of it?'

'We wish to convey to you, sir, something to your ad-vantage,' Mr Augustus Grimm senior continued.

Beaumont relaxed a little. He had never been called sir in his life, except by a police officer: 'Please blow into this breathalyser, sir.'

'Okay, Guv, what're you sellin'?' he asked.

'Are you the son of a George Robin Kyle Beaumont…' began Mr Augustus Grimm junior.

'… and the grandson of a Daniel Christopher George Beaumont?' Mr Oswald Grimes added. The three lawyers were like a double act, plus one.

'Erm, yes, that's me alright. What's this 'bout? Something to my advantage?' Pound signs popped into his head. *Lawyers always said, 'Something to your advantage' when loads of cash were on offer.*

Clearing his throat, Mr Grimm senior said, 'Well, Mr Beaumont, provided your father was legally married to your mother… erm… one Sadie Starling,' he consulted his notes, 'you, sir, are the heir to a title. We have traced the marriage certificates of all your ancestors from the third son of the Third Duke of Bartonshire, except your father's.' He cleared his throat again before continuing. 'Erm, are they legally married?' asked Mr Grimm senior discretely whispering.

''Course they are. Married fifty years weren't they, until me Da died that is. All legal an' in church an' all. "In the sight of God and this congregation", as they say,' Charlie Beaumont said.

'Where did that take place?' asked Mr Grimes.

'What's-its-name down the Old Kent Road, C of E, that's where. 'Ere, Mum, where was you and Dad hitched? What was the church called?' Charlie Beaumont called to a rather plump, red-faced woman who was behind a neighbouring stall selling knick-knacks to supplement her pension. She attended

16

local house clearances when someone died. Her ears had been listening to proceedings intently, catching words like 'heir' and 'title'. She too was thinking *money!*

'That church what has not seen either of us since you mean, 'cept when we buried your daddy?' said the woman, known as Mrs Sadie Beaumont, Charlie's mother. A formidable lady indeed!

'Yes, that one,' Charlie Beaumont replied.

'"Parish Church of Anne Askew, the Martyr", innit?' she declared. This was a small parish church in a poor district almost forgotten by time. 'Some girl what got tortured and burned at the stake way back. Seems she was burnt hereabouts. She was the first Englishwoman to demand a divorce, she was. Now there's an example to follow, Daisy Beaumont,' Sadie declared laughing to Charlie's wife who was nearby. 'Rector is a new bloke, Reverend Henderson or Anderson or something.'

Mr Grimm senior said, 'Then if you will excuse us, we must proceed there forthwith and check that out, just to confirm it you understand.' He doffed his bowler hat and left without another word. Mr Grimm junior and Mr Grimes did likewise and followed in his wake. The gathered crowd, mouths agape, parted like the Red Sea to let them through. It was like a scene from an 'Ealing Comedy' film.

Charlie Beaumont, his wife and mother stared at each other, speechless. Then they started dancing around swinging each other by the arms and singing, ♪*We're in the mon-ey, we're in the mon-ey!*♪

All the other folk in the market gathered round and joined in the celebration. 'How much lolly do you get?' asked someone.

'Dunno yet, but it's bound to be loads, with a title an' all,' said the mother. 'Imagine us in a mansion probably. Duke of Bartonshire he is! Wherever that is.'

'In Wales somewhere, isn't it?' someone remarked.

'Nah, it's up in t' north, in Scotland somewhere,' said another.

'You're thinking of Dumbarton,' said the first speaker. 'It is defo in Wales. Probably full of places with unpronounceable names.'

No one noticed Alfie "Sticky Fingers" Holmes, a small weasel-like person, surreptitiously helping himself to the contents of some of the cash boxes behind a few unattended stalls!

Chapter 2
The Tenth Duke of Bartonshire

'Oi, where's all me cash gone?' cried a stallholder when things quietened down, and he returned to work.

'Mine's gone too,' another shouted. Suddenly there was utter pandemonium. A dozen stalls had been robbed.

"Sticky Fingers" had long departed, however. *Mus' be me birfday,* he thought, laughing. *Gonna be a grand night down the Fox and Hounds tonight! Might even buy a round! Mus' get the missus some flowers: roses and stuff! Keep 'er sweet. It pays t' keep 'er sweet! Anything for a quiet life, Alfie boy. An' a box o' Dairy Milk chocs… a huge box. She'll love that, she will.* And he started to whistle "Who wants to be a millionaire?", as he walked jauntily down the street.

'Must have been when we were all dancing,' said Sadie Beaumont. 'Some rotten swine.'

'Don't fret,' shouted Charlie Beaumont, 'I'll see you are all okay once I get me fortune.' Folk were a bit comforted at this. No point in calling the cops! Most were dodging the taxman! 'Write your names on this here piece of paper an' approximately how much you think you lost,' Charlie continued. They all did so, though the estimates of losses were just a little exaggerated, in fact, a great deal exaggerated if truth be told.

Charlie Beaumont was aged thirty-three, of average height; his brown hair was receding rapidly at the front, leaving a sort of widow's peak, and he was several kilos overweight: a large belly and a missing shirt button or two testified to that. He wore a grubby checked shirt, sleeves rolled up, revealing several badly executed tattoos obtained, when much younger, on holiday in some foreign resort with his mates, "Chalky" White and "Bruiser" Barnes who never won a fight and had two cauliflower ears to prove it. Some tattoos were so rude, his girlfriend at the time insisted he had them amended. He also wore a baggy pair of corduroy trousers, a pair of old "Doc Martens" boots, and his previously mentioned apron which needed washing. In fact, it had needed washing two weeks ago. 'It'll chuck it in the wash another day,' he kept saying.

Presently, the three lawyers returned.

'Ah, Mr Beaumont, or should I say, Your Grace?' said Mr Grimm senior doffing his hat again. Every ear in the market was listening but keeping an eye on their cash this time. 'We have obtained a satisfactory confirmation of the marriage from the church records, and we are now pleased to declare you to be the Tenth Duke of Bartonshire!' Everyone cheered. (Several previous dukes had died young in various wars.)

Charlie Beaumont looked around him beaming from ear to ear. Some of his friends did overly elaborate bows and curtsies like they had seen on films. 'Wow, me an actual, real-life duke. Do I have a Coat of Arms an' stuff?' he asked the lawyers.

'Yes, you most certainly do, Your Grace. The Beaumont Family Arms are, if I recall correctly: *"Argent, on a Hill Vert a Lion Rampant Gules, supported by two French Prisoners of War, enchained",'* said Mr Grimm junior. Mr Grimes and Mr Grimm senior nodded in agreement.

'It's mostly Norman French you know,' said Mr Grimm senior helpfully.

Mr Grimes added, 'In English, it means: A silver shield, with a green hill or mountain, from the French *Beau,* beautiful, and *Mont,* mountain, one assumes, on which stands a red lion rampant, that is standing on its hind legs.'

'Somewhat like the Peugeot car logo actually. The prisoners in chains seem to have been from the Duke's sense of humour if one may call it that. He fought the French you know,' Mr Grimm junior said.

'Ooo, really nice too,' said Charlie Beaumont. 'I always knew Beaumont was a noble name. Norman-French an' all. Cool. An' the Duke was a war hero, you say! My ancestor was a war hero.' He strutted around looking noble. Folk again did lots of bowing and curtsying. One wag threw his anorak down in front of Charlie, like Sir Walter Raleigh is reputed to have done for Queen Elizabeth I.

'You could, of course, request the "College of Heraldry" to devise a new Coat of Arms should you wish. The family Latin motto, by the way, is *"Ut Non Segnes Efficiamini"*, which translates roughly "Be not slothful",' said Mr Grimm junior. 'From the Bible, somewhere.'

'The Book of the Letter to the Hebrews chapter six, verse twelve, I believe,' said Mr Grimm senior, matter-of-factly. He was a stickler for correct facts.

'Well, us Beaumonts aren't slothful, that's for sure,' said Charlie. 'Work all hours we do.'

'What about the fortune?' Mrs Sadie Beaumont demanded. She was not interested in red lions, green hills, nor Coats of Arms, much less Latin mottoes.

'Shall we adjourn to your residence, Your Grace, so we can discuss matters, in private?' Mr Grimm senior looked around at all the eager faces.

'Jack, will you look after me and Mum's stalls for a while?' Charlie asked a friend.

'Sure, Charlie, erm, Duke, no problem,' replied Jack, pleased he was now the trusted friend of a duke. Raised his street cred a few notches.

Once in the Beaumonts' tiny house not far away in Gasworks Street, Charlie's wife, Daisy, served tea in the best china quickly hauled from a cabinet. It had been a wedding present from Charlie's Aunt Maisy and never used till now. Some biscuits were also produced.

Charlie asked, 'Just how much dosh have I, we, got then?'

'Erm, unfortunately not a lot, sir,' said Mr Grimes. Faces looked glum.

'To be exact, the sum of nine hundred and fifty…' Mr Grimm senior began.

'Million? Nine hundred and fifty million quid?' Charlie gasped. 'That'll do nicely!' He rubbed his hands together. Sadie and Daisy nearly fainted.

'… pounds, and sixty-five pence,' Mr Grimm senior concluded. There was complete silence. Was that a pin dropping? No one breathed for several seconds. Never had the two Mrs Beaumont, mother and wife, been so silent. Charlie was, in modern parlance, completely gob-smacked!

'A lousy nine hundred an' fifty pounds, sixty-five lousy pence! You have got to be joking!' Daisy spoke for the first time. 'Trust you, Charlie Beaumont to inherit a title an' a lousy nine hundred an' fifty quid.'

'An' a lousy sixty-five pence,' Sadie added in disgust. Her face grimaced.

'Is that all?' Charlie asked hopefully. 'What about chests of jewels an' gold an' stuff? Dukes an' Earls an' such always have chests of gold coins an' gold plates in the dungeon, or secret hiding places, don't they? I've seen it on the telly.'

'Sorry, Your Grace, but there is no dungeon, no chests of gold, and no fortune in jewels. That is the stuff of fairy tales, I'm afraid. You see the late Duke was, shall we say, a gambler, to be exact, a rather poor gambler by all accounts, and with taxes etc., the family fortune has, erm, dwindled somewhat,' said Mr Grimes.

'"Dwindled somewhat"! If he wasn't already dead, I would kill him!' declared Sadie Beaumont.

'So, the family of the late Duke put the house up for sale and emigrated to Canada. Or they would have if the ship hadn't unfortunately sunk,' continued Mr Grimes.

'Yeah, I remember that. Dreadful disaster,' Charlie commented.

'Plus, death duty tax had to be paid on what the late duke had left. The house was taken off the market pending these enquiries as to an heir. You may dispose of it as you wish, of course,' said Mr Grimes.

'House? So, there is a house! How big a house, exactly?' Daisy asked, brightening.

Sadie grumbled, 'Knowing our luck, it will be a tumbled down cottage, with no roof!'

'A mansion one could call it, listed Grade One, but…' began Mr Grimm junior.

'Wow, a real mansion. Things are not so bad after all. Where is it, Mr Grimm?' Duke Charlie asked.

'It is called "Barton Hall", in Bartonshire of course. Quite small as mansions go. One hundred and fifty or so rooms, if you include the old servants' rooms, most with *en suite* bathrooms – except the old servants' rooms of course.'

'Oh, on sweet bathrooms… lovely,' declared Sadie with enthusiasm.

Mr Grimm junior continued, 'There are several bathrooms on the upper storey, however. It was extensively renovated and modernised inside and out by the Eighth Duke some years ago,' Mr Grimm senior stated. 'It comprises a rather elegant entrance hall with marble columns, four main reception rooms, plus a dining room, several smaller rooms including a library, minus books alas; the late duke was not a great reader, and a music room, *sans* instruments, several bedrooms – I haven't counted them – numerous former servants' bedrooms on the upper floor, as I have mentioned; about a half-mile of corridors, plus extensive old stables and outbuildings etc.

'Unfortunately, the Ninth Duke was, as we said, an ardent gambler. It is rumoured he once wagered ten thousand pounds that it would snow in central London on the fifteenth of July. He lost. There was a heat wave!'

'Land? How much land?' asked Daisy being practical. 'You cannot have a mansion without land.'

'One thousand acres approximately, and a large lake,' Mr Grimm senior replied. 'I'm afraid most of the land was sold off to clear some of his gambling debts and taxes. The Dukedom used to comprise about a third of Bartonshire!'

'What was the old fool betting on? Three-legged horses or donkeys or what?' Sadie asked sarcastically.

'Or some old nags about twenty years old, ready for the dog food factory?' added Daisy.

'Oh well. Could be worse. Where is Bartonshire anyway? Wales? I'm not good at geography,' said Charlie.

'You're not good at anything, Charlie Beaumont, not even inheriting dukedoms,' muttered Daisy.

'Yeah, someone said it is in Wales,' said Sadie.

Mr Grimes pretended not to have heard Daisy's remark. 'You go through Oxfordshire, and on a bit, then turn right. Use sat-nav if you have it.' (Charlie's old van did not possess satellite navigation. It did not even possess a working radio. In fact, it was a surprise when it started each morning).

'I'll give you the address,' said Mr Grimes. 'Here are the keys and the deeds. I suggest you lodge the deeds with a solicitor. And the best of luck.' *You will need it,* he thought. He handed over a large folder crammed with papers and several large iron keys on a ring.

Once they were back in their car, Mr Grimes said, 'We should have described the condition of the property, Augustus.'

'I was about to, Oswald, but I was interrupted by the duke,' said Mr Grimm junior. 'They will find out soon enough.' He smiled to himself.

Chapter 3
Market Barton, a Small City
in Central England

Two days later at the weekend, the Beaumont clan: Charlie, his wife Daisy, their children, Fred, dark hair (uncombed), then aged nine, and Maisy, seven and a half, with red hair and freckles, and of course his mum Sadie, piled into the family van, a little green Ford, which stank of fish, with a large salmon and the legend "Charles Beaumont and Son, Purveyors of Fresh Fish" painted on the side, and set off for the aforementioned mysterious Bartonshire.

It might have been Mongolia for all the Beaumonts knew of it. None of the clan had ever passed an examination in school, certainly not geography.

Sadie had an RAC roadmap on her lap and was doing navigator. 'Turn right, no left, no right, at the next crossroad.' Charlie was inclined to ignore her, *following his nose,* as he called it.

'Are we nearly there, yet?' Fred whined after about twenty minutes. He emphasised the word "yet".

'We are not out of London, yet. Sit there and be quiet,' his mother growled. Fred went into a sulk and resumed playing at his smartphone game.

'I'm hungry!' declared Maisy, five minutes later.

'You got your breakfast only a few minutes ago like the rest of us. You'll have to wait till we get there like everyone else,' said her mother, frowning. Maisy folded her arms and sulked. She could win gold medals for sulking. *"And now we have in first place in the Sulking Championship of Great Britain… Miss Maisy Beaumont."*

'Are we nearly there, yet?' was repeated every ten minutes or so of the journey.

Eventually, they were out in the country, the children were not interested, and they drove through Oxfordshire and on a bit. By lunchtime, they arrived in the sleepy county town of Market Barton, Bartonshire. Anything exciting rarely happened in the city. The last major event was in 1885 when Queen Victoria passed through on a train.

Market Barton was a small, pretty city in central England. Flower baskets hung from every lamppost and flowerbeds competed for attention. Not that the junior travellers were interested.

'Hmm, a bit better looking than London, I think. Very pretty,' said Sadie. Any plant she ever had was condemned to a quick death. A row of withered specimens on the kitchen windowsill bore witness. If there were a National Society for the Prevention of Cruelty to Plants, Sadie would have had a visit.

Near the city centre, St Oswald and St Theobald's Cathedral, the fourth largest in England, stood on a low hill overlooking the upper reaches of the River Thames, which ran through the southern part of the county. It was a large, mainly twelfth-century edifice in the traditional cruciform style, with three slender spires. At the crossing, atop a square tower, was a broach spire which carried upwards by means of triangular faces. The Victorians had added two similar spires at the west entrance: some of the more enhancing additions.

'I'm starving,' whined Fred, ignoring everything.

'Me too,' said Maisy. Her tummy rumbled. Fred's followed her lead.

'We'll stop at a café and get dinner, or maybe we should call it "luncheon" now we are nobility,' said Sadie. 'I suppose you two kids will be Lord Frederick and Lady Maisy or something. I'll have to check that with the lawyers.'

'Little Lord Fauntleroy maybe,' laughed Daisy. Fred grimaced.

Food, at last! I don't care what you call it, and I don't want to be Lady anything either, Maisy thought to herself.

'I don't care what it is called. I just need food, or I'll die on you,' Fred exaggerated. 'Then you'll be sorry. You'll be had up for murder. "LORD FRED STARVED TO DEATH BY UNCARING PARENTS", the headlines will say.' Fred was what is called "borderline obese" these days. He had in fact crossed the border! But as he played football, he at least got some exercise.

They stopped at the "Kosy Korner Kafé" on High Street to feed their faces. Fred made a face when he read the spelling. *Pretty naff,* he thought. Charlie later asked the waitress where Barton Hall was.

'Where it has always been,' came the waitress's smart reply, winking at the kids. Maisy giggled. Fred doubled up with laughter.

'Ha-ha, very funny,' Charlie replied with a smile.

The waitress giggled and gave them directions.

No one asked if he was the new duke, not even when he put on a posh accent, much to his disappointment. *Peasants, the lot of them! Off with their heads,* he thought and smiled to himself.

They drove on through the city passing a grand statue of the late Colonel Harold (Harry) Francis Christopher Harris, DSO & bar MC MM MiD AM First Class, of the Royal Bartonshire Light Infantry, a local war hero. Harris had served throughout World War II and went on to become the Colonel of the Regiment in 1950. His exploits in the war were a local legend. Many a discussion was heard in the local public houses concerning what he did. (Rumour had it he assassinated Hitler! But it was never confirmed. The War Department never responded to enquiries.) He died in 1995 leaving a widow and four grown-up children.

They continued until they came to a high stone wall on the left side of the road with a set of large pillars supporting black wrought iron gates, more than slightly rusted, and a rather derelict gate lodge. Some of the roof slates had blown off in a storm. A makeshift sign with the legend "Barton Hall" hung precariously by a single nail on a wall. *We will have to get this lot sorted,* thought Charlie.

'This must be it,' declared Maisy, as they drove up to the gates. 'A bit tatty looking if you ask me.' "Tatty" was her current favourite word: *My book is tatty. Those curtains look tatty,* etc.

'We'll soon put that right,' Charlie declared. *I hope the mansion is in better condition,* he thought. He was beginning to have doubts. They were all beginning to have doubts.

Fred opened the gates and Charlie drove up a long driveway between numerous mature chestnut and beech trees planted in the eighteenth century, until they rounded a bend and got their first view of the "Hall".

'Wow! It's huge,' Fred said, showing interest for the first time. 'It must be as big as Buckingham Palace.' He exaggerated a little as usual.

'Yes, isn't it,' said Charlie, 'and it's all ours! The Beaumonts have arrived.'

'Driveway is tatty and full of potholes and weeds,' said Daisy.

We'll soon sort that out too, thought Charlie. 'Don't worry about weeds and potholes. We'll soon sort that out,' Charlie said. The list of things that needed "sorting" was growing rapidly.

'Oh, look over to the right, there's the lake. Isn't it just so beautiful!' Sadie declared. A large expanse of blue water glittered in the sun. 'It's like a scene from a film.'

A large Georgian style mansion, three storeys high, with seemingly countless windows and chimneys, faced them as they rounded a bend. The cream-coloured stonework of the façade almost glowed in the afternoon sunshine. Two rows of large windows marked the lower floors and a row of dormer windows in the slated roof defined the top floor. Larger rooms at each end gave the appearance of towers with crenelated decoration along the top.

'Wow!' they all said as one and sat spellbound for a few minutes when Charlie stopped the van.

'It's like a fairy tale castle,' said Maisy.

They then drove right up to the front of the house, where the driveway curved round a sort of ornamental roundabout with a statue, in the centre, of a scantily clad Roman or Greek maiden, in flowing drapery, carrying an urn on her shoulder. She was partly covered in moss and lichen.

'Ooo, you can see her…' Fred began to say with a grin.

'FREDERICK BEAUMONT! Don't you dare!' his mother shouted, and she put her hands over Maisy's ears, then over her eyes, then back over her ears. *Disgusting! That'll have to go,* she thought.

Fred was only called "Frederick" when he had done something bad, and "Frederick Beaumont" when he had done something extremely bad.

'…armpit. I was going to say armpit,' Fred laughed. Daisy frowned and Charlie glared at him.

'Okay, everyone out and stretch your legs,' Charlie said. He already felt so duke-like.

The building formed a large rectangle with a courtyard about the size of four tennis courts in the centre. This had become overgrown with weeds and dead leaves, as they eventually discovered. Each window had about twelve panes of glass, and each chimney, of which there were many, had about eight or ten chimneypots. Or would have had if some had not been broken or missing! Rooks had built nests on some, and tree seedlings had rooted in places. The place was a mess to say the least.

A flight of granite steps about twenty feet wide descended from a terrace at the front of the building, and then split right and left to narrower flights of steps curving down to the driveway. Stone urns ornamented each junction. The wide terrace was edged with a stone balustrade, also mostly moss-covered.

The intrepid explorers started to climb the steps. *It's like being Indiana Jones,* Fred thought. He had a vivid imagination. Weeds were growing in every nook and cranny. Fred kicked the "clock" off a dandelion. Maisy picked one and blew on it to tell the time.

'It's four o'clock,' she stated with certainty.

'No, it's not, it's half-past one,' Fred laughed. 'You should blow harder.' Maisy ignored him.

'Like I said, it is all a bit tatty,' said Maisy dismissively.

'Bit o' elbow grease will soon sort that lot,' Daisy affirmed decisively.

'What's elbow grease when it's at home?' Fred asked.

'Never mind,' said Charlie and gave Fred a nudge up the steps.

'Ouch! That hurt!' he moaned. He had learned when playing football to exaggerate every knock, usually rolling around on the pitch in "pain". Professional players have a lot to answer for.

When they reached the top of the steps and stood on the wide paved terrace that stretched the length of the front of the mansion, they were more than a bit taken aback. Many windows had broken panes replaced with wood or hardboard. Lumps of masonry, which had fallen from the roof parapet, littered the ground.

'Oh look, a huge lawn,' cried Maisy looking through the pillars of the stone balustrade.

'Hmm, it would be a lawn if the grass weren't a foot high,' Fred grunted. So far, he had seen nothing too pleasing. 'And I'm not mowing it. No fear,' he said. 'It'll take a month to mow that lot!'

'Oi, who be you lot then?' said a loud voice, in a local accent strange to London ears, not too politely for the speaker was suspecting thieves. He suspected everyone of being a potential thief or vandal, an "undesirable" as he called them. He had been known to fire off a shot or two from his shotgun, in the air of course. It had the desired effect of scaring off undesirables.

They all were startled and jumped and looked round to see who had spoken. A grizzled little man in a tweed jacket with leather elbow patches and carrying a shotgun under his arm, as he had been shooting crows, had come around the corner of the building. He wore a pair of green wellington boots.

Charlie spoke. 'I be… erm… I am the new Duke of this here place. Charlie Beaumont's the name.'

'Oh yes, the lawyer chap, Grimes, told me to expect a new Duke. Pleased to meet Your Grace, I'm sure,' Harry said doffing his cap. 'I be Harry Grimsdale, the caretaker of this here mansion. Part-time that is. I tries t' keep the local youths away best I can. They'll steal anything not nailed down, they will! And I won't embarrass the ladies by saying what else I found!' Harry made a disgusted face. Fred began to wonder what Harry meant.

'Just call me Charlie, Harry. This here beautiful lady is my wife Daisy, my kids, Fred and Maisy, and my mum Sadie,' Charlie introduced his family. They all nodded in turn. Harry gave a nod to each in turn.

'Pleased t' meet you all,' said Harry shaking hands with Charlie. 'Like I said, the local youths have done a bit o' damage, but I boarded up the windows best I could. I can't be here all the time. I've got me own little farm t' look after.' He was being modest. It was quite a large farm, dairy mainly, with its own milk pasteurisation and bottling plant.

'By the way, I haven't been paid for two weeks for me caretaking.' In fact, it was one week, but Harry took the opportunity to bolster his finances.

'Hmm, the lawyers never mentioned you. How much are you owed, then?' asked Charlie.

'Oh, hundred and ten quid should cover it,' Harry said without hesitating.

'Well, if you are owed, we had better see you right,' Charlie said. 'Can't have folk saying the new duke is mean, can we?' He carefully counted out ten ten-pound notes and two fivers. *That's a chunk of my inheritance gone already,* he thought. Sadie and Daisy were thinking the same thing. Fred just thought, *That would buy a load of chocolate.*

'Sorry, but we shan't be needing your services any longer, Mr Grimsdale,' said Sadie decisively. *Rob us blind he will,* she was thinking. *He'll be wanting a pay-rise next, or a pension.* Harry's little deception had backfired on him.

Harry looked disgruntled but said nothing. He would be telling the locals down in the "Pig and Whistle" that evening how nasty the new duke's people were. He pocketed the cash, muttered, 'I'll bid you all good day,' and stalked off.

'Oh dear, I think we have made an enemy there,' Daisy commented.

'I hope not,' said Charlie, glaring at his mother. 'We need the goodwill of the locals if we are to make this a success.'

Sadie just shrugged her shoulders. *They'll all be coming around, all smarmy, to meet the new duke, I'm sure,* she thought.

Chapter 4
'We've Been Robbed!'

'Let's get inside and have a look around,' said Fred. He had stopped using his smartphone game at last.

'Okay, here goes,' said Charlie, and he produced the large iron keys on a ring from a coat pocket. They all walked up to the ornate pedimented entrance, with four Mourne granite pillars. The family Coat of Arms and motto were carved in stone above the door. *Hmm, I don't think we will be changing that,* Charlie thought. He inserted the key in the lock. *We will need a few of these keys made, or find a different entrance,* he thought. He turned the key with some effort. The heavy oak door creaked open with a loud *creeaaak* sound. Fred gave the large iron knocker, in the shape of a lion's head, a good tap. It echoed around the interior.

'It is like one of them there Dracula films,' commented Daisy.

'Oooooo,' Fred noised like a ghost. Maisy squealed and clung to her mother.

'Frederick, behave!' the mother shouted, clipping his ear.

If the Beaumonts were expecting walls hung with Rembrandts, Constables and Titians, they were soon disappointed. Not that any of them had ever heard of Rembrandt, Constable or Titian. On the walls, there were only large rectangles of unfaded wallpaper and cobwebs where paintings had once hung. Much of the wallpaper was peeling off and the floor was covered in dust and rubbish.

'Robbed! We've been robbed!' wailed Sadie. 'The place has been robbed! Some security that bloke provided. Good money, down the drain.'

'They've probably all been sold for paying the gambling debts. That idiot relative of mine! I'll check with the lawyers when we get home,' Charlie said.

'Still, who wants a load of ol' paintings anyway?' said Sadie, trying to put a brave face on it.

The entrance hall was immense, with black and white tiled patterns on the floor. Six marble pillars supported the upper floors. A large chandelier, covered in a dust sheet, hung above the centre, in the middle of a ceiling painted with scenes of Italian countryside. Obviously, no one wanted to buy a chandelier that size! A couple of marble plinths, which presumably used to hold statues, were at the bottom of the grand staircase that ascended in a sweeping curve to the right of the door.

To one side of the hall sat an extremely large brass gong suspended from the trunk of a wooden elephant.

Presumably, no one wished to buy it either, as it would be difficult to fit through the door of a modern house! The children made a beeline for it of course, with predictably noisy results.

'You can quit that for a start!' shouted Charlie. Everyone had their hands over their ears.

'Aw, Dad,' moaned Fred.

'Don't "Aw, Dad" me, Frederick!' Charlie only used "Frederick" when he was annoyed. 'Do what you're told for once!' Fred made a face when no one was looking.

'Let's go exploring,' Maisy suggested.

'Yeah, that will be fun,' Fred replied.

'Well, don't go far and be careful. We don't know what the floorboards might be like. Could be dry rot or anything,' Daisy said feeling rather pessimistic. She had visions of children's legs appearing through the ceiling.

The two kids scampered off up the curving oak and mahogany staircase. Fred thought he might have a go at sliding down the bannisters when the olds were not watching. He had the feeling they would object. The olds always spoiled his fun.

'Look at the state of this place: paper peeling off the walls, little furniture, no 'lectric,' said Sadie trying a light switch. 'No heating probably, an' bits falling off the roof.' What furniture there was left was covered in dustsheets. She uncovered a chair and sat down gloomily. Dust flew everywhere.

'But it's ours, all ours, to do with as we wish,' Charlie said cheerfully, though he felt anything but cheerful.

'We don't need to do everything at one go. We can get a few bedrooms and the kitchen in order, clean up a bit, get the 'lectric back on, all that sort of stuff, and then plan the rest,' suggested Daisy.

'Daisy's right, as always. A bit of a clean-up will make a huge difference,' said Charlie giving his wife a kiss on the cheek. He lifted the receiver on an old black "dial" telephone… dead as a doornail.

'First things first. Mum, phone the electric company on your mobile; there's an old phone book over there, and the water department and get us back online. Say something like,

"His Grace, the Duke, requires reconnection urgently".' Charlie put on a posh accent. Sadie laughed.

'Daisy, find the kitchen and see what it's like, and I'll check out a few bedrooms. Three will do to start. The kids will have to share for a while.'

Twenty minutes later, they all sat on the bottom stair and reported. 'The 'lectric and water will be turned on as soon as their men arrive with the agreement papers. When I mentioned you were the new duke, Charlie, they couldn't have been more obliging. Titles still pull weight,' said Sadie. 'I pretended I was your secretary, all posh like.'

Daisy said, 'The kitchen is huge. There is a big old Aga cooker, but also an electric cooker with six hotplates, which will do us. As far as I can tell, the Aga cooker heats the water, so we will need to get it lit sometime. Plenty of crockery and stuff as well, with our Coat of Arms on it would you believe!'

'An Aga will hardly heat enough water for all the bathrooms in this place. There must be another way. Anyway, the beds look okay. Lovely thick mattresses. Luckily, they weren't sold. Fourposter beds are a bit big for houses these days, I suppose. We will need duvets, pillows and things, and towels. You kids will have to share for a while,' said Charlie. Fred had put off the proposed banister-sliding because the olds were present.

'Aw, Dad, I want a room of my own!' Fred whined.

'I'm not sharing with a boy! Especially not our Freddie. His feet are really yuck,' Maisy said, making a face, and she folded her arms determinedly. "Yuck" was another word in vogue.

'There's nothing wrong with my feet!' Fred protested. 'I wash them every week, whether they need it or not,' he chuckled. Maisy made a face and stuck out her tongue.

'You'll do as you are told. We can sort out more rooms in due course, if we decide to stay,' Charlie said in a voice that allowed no contradiction.

'The children could use two of the old servants' rooms on the top floor. I noticed they are smaller,' suggested Sadie.

'Yeah! Cool!' said Fred and Maisy in unison.

'When we return, we must open a few windows to air the bedrooms,' said Daisy.

'But what are we going to do with this big place? We cannot afford to repair and maintain it. It will cost thousands of pounds… which we don't have, seeing as you only inherited a few hundred,' said Sadie. 'And there are so many rooms! We will never need all of them, and I am certainly not cleaning them all! We don't have droves of servants.'

'Let's think about it on the way back to London,' said Charlie. 'There is no hurry.' He was really getting the hang of being a duke and being decisive.

'We could apply for grants an' stuff, from them folk what look after old houses,' suggested Sadie.

'Yeah, I've seen them on the telly. The lawyers said it was listed Grade One,' Daisy added. 'That means any repairs have to be: "sympathetic to the original architecture",' she quoted. 'I've seen it on the telly,' she repeated, to emphasise the point.

'Hey, I've just thought, if there is a coronation, we would be invited as the Duke and Duchess of Bartonshire. Just think!' declared Charlie. 'I'll need a… what-do-you-call-it? A duke's coronet and a cloak.'

'You would have to shave first, Charlie Beaumont,' Daisy laughed. 'An' I would need a tiara an' posh frock. I'm not going to Westminster Abbey in my usual frocks.' She mimed putting a tiara on her head and walked around with her head held high. Everyone laughed.

Just then, the men from the electric and water companies arrived. The men wondered how this scruffy little man could be the Duke but proceeded to get the documents completed.

'Electric will be on in a jiffy,' said one.

'I'll turn on t' water now. I know where it connects t' the mains,' said the other and he wandered off round the building. Meanwhile, Charlie took some photographs to show the folk back in London.

'Okay, everyone, back in the van,' said Sadie, when all was sorted, and she headed for the door.

Before they left, Charlie lifted a large piece of discarded hardboard and took it with him as he locked the door. 'This will need its hinges oiled,' he muttered.

Once in the van, he found a marker pen he used for adverts on his market stall and wrote on the hardboard.

He drove back down the driveway and stopped at the main road. After closing the rusty gates, more oil needed, he tied the sign on a gate. It read:

TRESPASSERS WILL BE EATEN BY DOGS OR SHOT!
SURVIVORS WILL BE PROSECUTED!
YOU HAVE BEEN WARNED!
BY ORDER, CHARLES BEAUMONT,
TENTH DUKE OF BARTONSHIRE.

He stepped back and admired his handiwork. 'That should keep the local yobs out, I hope.'

Fred had helped with the spelling: "ATE" had been enlarged to "EATEN", and he added the punctuation. Charlie had not a clue about punctuation.

'I've never needed anything punctured in my life,' he declared.

Chapter 5
'You Can't Be a Proper Duke an' Live in a Two-Up Two-Down!'

Silence reigned for most of the journey back to London. Everyone had put their thinking caps on, except Maisy. Maisy fell asleep. Fred just felt hungry again, even though they had stopped for sandwiches and drinks in the city as they passed through.

Then Daisy suggested, 'Maybe we should just sell it. Bound to be worth a million or two. I mean, I saw an old tumbled down cottage on TV for sale for almost a quarter of a million! Some folk will buy any old thing.'

'Yeah, we can sell it to a millionaire pop star or something,' said Fred. *Or some other prat with money to spend,* he thought.

'Or get a film crew in like that place in "Downton Abbey" or whatever it was called, on the telly. I bet they got thousands for the use of that place,' said Sadie. 'Tourists come to see places what have been on the telly.'

'We could move in and renovate it gradually. I'm pretty handy at painting an' stuff,' said Charlie. 'Besides, what's the point of being a duke what has no mansion? You can't be a proper duke an' live in a two-up, two-down in Gasworks Street!'

'An' just what is wrong with Gasworks Street?' asked Sadie defensively. 'I was born and raised there don't forget, an' your grandparents before me.'

'Nothing wrong with it, it is just not a duke sort of place,' Charlie said laughing.

'We could apply for a mortgage,' said Daisy.

'That's a good idea. I'll see the nearest bank manager when we get back to Market Barton,' Charlie said.

'If we move there, I'll miss all my pals,' chirped Fred.

'Me too,' added Maisy, who had wakened.

'I'm on the Gasworks United under elevens football team now,' Fred added for effect. He was a goalkeeper because he was too slow at running. The team was still called after the old gasworks though it had been closed years ago.

'You'll make new friends soon enough, an' get on a new team,' said Daisy.

More silence, except for the rattles of the van.

'Guests! What about using the ground floor rooms for bed an' breakfast guests?' Daisy suggested.

'That's a grand idea, Duchess,' said Charlie laughing. They all laughed and began to sing, ♫*It's a long way to Market Barton. It's a long way to go. It's a long way to Market Barton to the biggest house I know.* ♫

Then, as they turned into Gasworks Street where they lived, Sadie exclaimed, 'What's that they say 'bout if you can't go to the mountain, bring the mountain to you? Something like that anyway. We could ask our friends to come and live in the Hall rent-free, just so long as they all pitch in and help with the work. Between us, we could repair it much cheaper an' raise money with different projects.'

'That's a great idea, Mum,' said Charlie. 'There's plenty of rooms for sure. We could ask folk what have special jobs like carpenter, plumber…'

'Or stonemason or chimney sweep. All them chimneys are bound to need sweeping,' said Daisy. 'And a glazier as well. We definitely need new glass. A lot of glass.'

'I'm not climbing up no chimney to sweep it. No fear,' Fred declared. He had heard about child chimney sweeps in school history class. The adults just ignored him.

And so, it was decided that next day, they would draw up a list of suitable people, and they went to bed dreaming of the high life.

Fred dreamed he was captain and leading scorer of course, of his new team, Barton Hall United. He was of course very slim and fit in his dream.

Ronaldo eat your heart out, Fred thought.

Chapter 6
'Any Slackers Will Be Turfed Out On Their Ear An' No Mistake.'

Next morning, the Beaumont house was buzzing. Everyone was up and about bright and early.

'Let's make a list of suitable people for the jobs we need,' said Charlie grabbing pen and paper.

'Hadn't we best ask all our friends? If we ask some an' not others, we could cause offence. I don't want to fall out with anybody,' Sadie said. 'I couldn't look them in the face.'

'That's true,' said Daisy, thoughtfully. 'We could lose many of our friends.'

'We'll not be here to know,' Fred chirped in. He was ignored. *Why can't we just stay here?* he thought.

'Okay, we will call a meeting of the folk what we know, an' let them volunteer. But making sure they all know that they must pull their weight, as far as work is concerned. Any slackers will be turfed out on their ear an' no mistake!' Charlie said decidedly. 'We can't afford to carry slackers.'

'We especially need tradesmen what can do all the repairs. They could also do jobs for the local carrot crunchers, erm, country people, to bring in some cash. And we could get those lawyers, Grimm and Grimmer, or whatever they're called, to draw up an agreement that everyone must sign up to,' said Sadie feeling clever.

'Right, we'll do that today. I'll phone them, an' then call a meeting in the parish hall for ten a.m. the day after tomorrow,' Charlie said decisively. He liked being decisive.

So, the rest of that day, the family spread the word, and all their friends and relatives spent that evening discussing whether to up stakes and move to Barton Hall. This caused great excitement in the neighbourhood.

Chapter 7
'Now, to Get to the Point...'

It is surprising, if not amazing, how quickly news spreads when loads of cash are thought to be in the offing! At ten a.m. on the appointed day, about two hundred people were assembled in the local parish hall. The clergyman, Rev. Percival Truesdale, was a bit unhappy at the thought of a number of his parishioners disappearing to the country, but he thought that as he only saw most of them at weddings or funerals (attending, or as the corpse), it hardly mattered.

He opened proceedings with a prayer for God's guidance for, "His Grace the Duke, the Duchess, family and friends".

'I don't know some of these people,' Charlie muttered to Daisy.

'Scroungers most likely. We can weed out the ones we don't know, or don't trust,' she replied out of the side of her mouth.

They need not have worried. Charlie stepped forward to applause, whistles and calls of, 'Here's the Duke.'

He tapped the mic. 'Friends, it is good to see you all here this morning.' The sound system squealed a bit. 'As you know, we have had a bit o' good news. I am now the Tenth

Duke of Bartonshire and this beautiful lady here is my beautiful wife, the new Duchess of Bartonshire.' Daisy blushed. Lots of clapping followed, and he waited for silence. *I am getting the hang of this speaking lark,* he thought.

'Now, to get to the point, we have been left this here mansion, "Barton Hall", what is huge. Freddie will hand round some photos.' Fred proceeded to do so. 'The problem is, as you can see, it needs a lot of work doing, and well, the last Duke didn't leave us much lolly. In fact, only a few hundred quid.' The promise to reimburse those who had had money stolen was conveniently forgotten. A lot of faces fell, and muttering began. Many chancers slipped away out of the hall seeing the prospect of easy money fly out of the window.

When things quietened down again, Charlie continued, 'What we have invited you, our friends, here for is to give you the chance of a lifetime: to move to Barton Hall rent-free...' much chatter ensued, 'provided...' he raised his hands and his voice to make himself heard, '... provided you are willing to pitch in and help with repairs an' stuff. If everyone is willing, as Mr Winston Churchill might have said, to do their bit of hard graft, we can do it and live like lords.' There was much nodding, but a lot of headshaking. The words "bit of hard graft" put many off. They had been hoping for a life of ease and luxury, servants and valets at their beck and call.

Who is this Churchill when he's at home? I must Google him, Fred thought.

''Ere, Charlie, your Dukeness, what are you going to be doing while we are doing all this hard graft?' shouted a voice from the back of the room.

'I shall be pitching in too, Bill Tubbs. I can help those as has skills like wood-working an' such. Those with skills are especially needed. There will be plenty to do, at least in the beginning. Well, for a few years.'

Sadie stood, grabbed the mic and added, 'Carpenters, plumbers, a chimney sweep; all sorts are needed. Oh, and cooks and someone to keep an eye on the kids. There will be a job for everyone.'

'What about schools? Are there any schools handy?' a young woman asked. 'I've got five little uns.'

'Yes, we saw schools in the city, so they aren't far away. Dead nice they looked an' all,' said Daisy.

'We have got them lawyers to draw up an agreement for us all to sign.' Charlie waved some sheets of paper. 'So, we all have the same rights and if necessary, and I am sure it won't be, we can chuck out any shirkers,' he said. A proviso he was later extremely glad he included.

'All money earned by work for the locals will go into a common purse so to speak. It will be like them there Pilgrim Fathers what went to America in... well, whenever it was. Freddie will know,' and he looked at Fred. Everyone looked at Fred.

Fred shook his head. 'Dunno, Dad. We have only done the stone-age an' bronze-age in school. Like that will be useful when I go for a job!' Fred grumbled. 'I don't imagine I'll ever be making a "wattle and daub" hut or a stone axe.'

'At least there will be no savage natives to fight off, just the carrot crunchers,' a voice added. Everyone laughed.

'Common purse? Sounds a bit too Commie to me,' muttered Davy Adamson and he left. *No one's getting their mitts on my cash,* he thought. 'Agreement! Bah!'

'We will give you a few days to think about it, and if all agree, we shall set sail within the next week or two.

'Oh, and there is a weekly market in Market Barton, as the name suggests, and surrounding towns for any who wish to do a bit of trading, and they have a good football team: Barton Wanderers, in League Two,' Charlie finished.

That appealed to many of his hearers, as trading and sport was all they knew.

Chapter 8
They Had to Make a Go of This

And so, on Monday morning, three weeks later, ten families turned up. Each had a van or car laden with everything but the kitchen sink. Those would have been there too if they could have been moved! There were beds, mattresses, clothing, tinned food, stocks of market goods, televisions, laptops, brooms, Hoovers, furniture, washing machines, spades, and tools of every description. Even a potter's kiln. Each person knew there would be no turning back. They had to make a go of this. Failure was out of the question. All had paid their rent up to date and gathered as much cash together as they could. It was a leap in the dark for them all.

'Wow, it is so wonderful to see you all,' said Charlie, with sincerity. The Beaumonts had feared no one would turn up. Several families had promised, dithered, and changed their minds, afraid to take the plunge.

'For those what have televisions, we can buy one licence to cover the whole house, instead of one each. We'll be quids in,' Charlie said jokingly.

'If we ever had TV licences!' a cheery voice shouted.

'Erm, maybe the least said about that the better,' said Charlie chuckling. 'But seriously, we must be careful to keep within the law, because there will be those who will want to bring us down, who would just love to see us fail.' Murmurs and nods of agreement.

'That's true enough,' said one person. 'We'll prove them wrong.'

'No more Burton to pay,' said Harry Dunlop who loved using Cockney rhyming slang.

'What?' asked Fred. 'Burton?'

'Burton-Upon-Trent, rent,' replied Harry. Fred grimaced, and then chuckled.

'Right then,' said Daisy. 'If you have read this agreement the lawyers have drawn up, form a queue to sign up then we can be on our way. Me, Charlie and Sadie have already signed.'

'It says in it, "A committee will oversee all matters",' said Mrs Higginson referring to the small print. 'What committee would that be?'

Charlie spoke with authority. 'Naturally, we will need some folk to make decisions about certain things, so there is no messin' about. The committee will be elected democratically by us all; by all, say, over eighteen anyway.'

'I want a vote,' said Fred loudly. He was ignored by the adults. *Some democracy,* he thought. He had read about democracy in an encyclopaedia in the school library; his teacher, Miss Wilkinson, having failed to explain it to his satisfaction. Most teachers failed to explain things to Fred's satisfaction as he had an insatiable curiosity.

'Sounds fair,' said Mrs Higginson and everyone nodded. Charlie breathed a sigh of relief, as he feared his "ship" was about to sink, torpedoed before the voyage had started by HMS Higginson.

The ten families that signed up were as follows:

1. The aforementioned, **Mrs Edith Higginson,** housewife and stallholder, good at knitting, sewing etc. 'I can sell my work on the stall.'
    Alexander Higginson, her husband, plumber/handyman (well under Edith's thumb). From Kent originally. +Two kids: Johnny and Kate.

2. **Lee Wu**, originally from Hong Kong, cook, good with accounts. (His café, "The Golden Dragon" had been bulldozed recently for redevelopment, so he decided to move using his compensation money.) 'Why we not give it a go?'
    Brenda Wu, housewife and cook. Secretary for an accountant prior to marriage. +Three kids: Samuel, Christopher, James.

3. **George McNeil**, carpenter, glazer and handyman. "Jack-of-all-trades". Originally from Belfast so he was.
    Annie McNeil, his wife, stallholder for children's clothing, cleaner and part-time shop assistant. Their only child died young.

4. **Thomas Jameson**, chimney sweep and window cleaner. 'I can turn my hand to anything.' He was from south London born and bred.
    Mildred Jameson, his wife, part-time primary school teacher (currently unemployed) + one kid, Tommy junior.

5. **Benjamin (Benny) Porter**, builder and mechanic, originally from Staffordshire. Was a fire fighter until a back injury brought a halt to that occupation.

Gwen Porter, very busy housewife! Likes decorating. +Five kids: Susan, Geoffrey, Lionel, Denver and Charlotte (who kept her busy).

6. **Quentin Lyttle,** glazer, painter-decorator and electrician. Originally from the West Indies. 'Give me the tools and I'll do the job, except mountain climbing. I hate heights, man.'

   Barbara Lyttle, his wife, shop assistant and painter-decorator with hubby. +One kid, a daughter, Arwen (Welsh for fair one). Barbara was originally from Wales' Rhondda Valley.

7. **Carol Dunlop**, a retired teacher. Londoner. 'I can look after the little ones.'

   Harry Dunlop, her husband of thirty-five years, aka *MacIntyre* (he had been *mackin'* tyres for years. Had worked in a tyre factory). Now a gardener (green fingers) and handyman. Also, a Cockney Londoner.

8. **Johnny Anderson**, a motor mechanic. 'Anything what I can do, I'll do it.' From east London.

   Olivia Anderson, his wife, stallholder and potter and artist. Hence the potter's kiln mentioned earlier.

9. **Uel Middleton**, security guard and bouncer at a nightclub. He was a big man. 'You want it done? I'm your man.'

   Mary Middleton, stallholder. Good with figures. 'She's a hard worker,' people said about her. Londoner like her husband. +Two kids Darren, Dwayne. (More about these two lads later).

10. **Dante Whittington** (his mother was keen on poetry) carpenter. 'Not afraid of grafting.'

Daphne-Isabelle Whittington. Housewife and nurse, temporarily out of work due to young kids. Both from Brighton originally. +Three kids: Lily and Rose, twins aged three, and older sister, Mary, five and a half (the half was important to Mary).

A total of twenty adults and seventeen children of various ages, plus the five members of the Beaumont clan set off for Market Barton. Oh, and assorted dogs, cats and budgerigars, and Arwen's rabbit, Snuggles.

A crowd had gathered to see them off, singing, ♪*For they are jolly good fellows.* ♪ Much cheering and flag-waving followed them down the street, as a procession of eleven vehicles set off, the Duke and Duchess's van leading the way. Kids had draped it in bunting. Everyone was excited, to put it mildly. A horde of young lads ran after them till the vehicles picked up speed.

'They'll be back, mark my words,' said Davy Adamson. 'It'll never work. I give 'em a month, tops! Pilgrim Fathers? Huh! Nonsense. If they don't return, I'll eat my 'at.'

His son Joey commented, 'You never wear an 'at, Da!' Davy just grunted.

'If anyone can make a go of this, it's Charlie,' said another man.

Chapter 9
Some People Thought
It Was a Circus

The procession stopped folk in their tracks whenever it passed. Some people thought it was a circus, others a hippy convoy. Others just stood open-mouthed in wonder and bewilderment, scratching their heads.

When they reached the outskirts of Oxford, they queued up at a filling station to refill the fuel tanks, and for "calls of nature". Fred made a beeline for the gents' toilet. The dogs were given short walks. The cats just found it all too boring and undignified, and continued sleeping, but some eyed the budgies. The budgies eyed the cats, and no doubt were glad they were securely in cat-boxes!

The shop assistant, Mildred Ashworth, was almost too surprised to comment, as the mob like a swarm of locusts, cleared the shelves of foodstuffs especially bread, milk and pet food. *Is this a robbery? Should I call the cops?* she thought.

'Where are all you folk off to then?' she asked as she put a pile of things through the checkout.

'We are moving to Bartonshire. Barton Hall to be exact,' said Daphne Whittington. 'That man there,' she pointed at Charlie, 'is the new duke!'

'Wow, I never seen me a real live duke before, 'cept on TV!' she replied, and was ever so polite to Charlie when he came to the till. *I wonder if he's married. I fancy being a duchess,* Mildred thought as she smiled sweetly and fluttered her eyelashes. Then Daisy appeared at his side, and clutched Charlie's arm making sure her wedding ring was clearly visible. *Oh well. Can't win 'em all,* the girl thought.

The city of Market Barton came to a standstill when the convoy arrived. Jaws hit the ground as astounded city-folk stopped in their tracks and lined the pavements. Charlie called a halt in the High Street in front of the rather grand Victorian City Hall, a large red brick building reached by a huge flight of steps.

Charlie raised a hand to get attention. 'Ladies and gentlemen, I am Charlie Beaumont, the new Duke of Bartonshire, and this is my lovely wife, Daisy, the new Duchess.' He put his arm around Daisy. 'My friends and I are moving into Barton Hall to renovate it. We will be inviting you all to visit as soon as we get settled in and get things shipshape. But bring your own grub,' he added, with a grin. Everyone laughed.

'Duke? You?' a fat man heckled loudly. 'Pull the other one, it's got bells on.' There was some laughter from the crowd, and a few people started to leave.

'Okay, I know I am a bit of a scruff,' Charlie shouted, 'but I was not born with a silver spoon in my gob. I am an ordinary working man just like you, so give us a chance.' Some folk started to applaud and then to cheer. The convoy folk waved back, and they then drove on to the Hall.

The temporary sign was still on the gate, and nothing appeared to have been moved. 'Looks like my sign worked,' said Charlie with a grin. *Let's hope so,* Daisy thought.

'Saved us a few quid on security anyway,' said Sadie.

Fred got out and opened the gate and they proceeded up the driveway. The newcomers gasped when they rounded a bend and they saw the house for the first time.

'Wow, they said it was big but… wow!' exclaimed Benny Porter. 'It's… like a palace.' When the convoy parked at the foot of the steps, they all got out and stood totally amazed.

'Right, first things first,' Charlie said loudly. 'We, the Duchess and I…' some laughter at Charlie's assumed posh accent… 'are terribly pleased and honoured to welcome you, one and all, to our little house in the country.' More laughter.

'Some little house!' exclaimed Dante Whittington.

Charlie continued in his normal voice. 'We have chosen rooms on the first floor for ourselves and Mum, which we have marked with post-it notes on the doors. The kids have rooms on the top floor. You can use the rooms on the top floor, which are smaller, for your older kids. If you now choose a room or rooms as needed for yourselves; they are huge, believe me. Open the windows to air the rooms, and then we can start unloading all our stuff. The ground floor rooms we are keeping vacant for possible paying guests, hopefully in the near future.' Everyone nodded in agreement.

'And you, kids, no sliding on banisters. We don't want any accidents! And do not go near the lake unless an adult is with you. We do not want any tragedies!' said retired teacher Mrs Dunlop with sternness. Disappointed faces on the kids.

'Typical adults,' Fred grumbled to himself. 'We never get allowed any fun.'

'An' leave the gong alone!' added Sadie. Fred and Maisy had told all the others of "the big elephant gong". More disappointed faces!

Huh, nothing has changed. Adults are <u>always</u> *the same: rotten spoilsports! I do wish we had stayed in London,* Fred thought grumpily.

Everyone ascended the steps to the front door and looked around with open-mouthed wonder.

'It's... huge... just enormous,' Olivia Anderson commented in wonder. All agreed with her, nodding their heads.

Charlie opened the door.

'Needs a drop of oil does that,' Alexander Higginson stated the obvious.

'Right, everyone, off you go up the stairs and find a bedroom.' There was an excited, noisy rush as they scrambled to be first.

'Wow! Look at the size of this bedroom. It's bigger than our whole house was in London!' Mary Middleton exclaimed. 'The windows are enormous! What a view! Hardly a house in sight. And the lake is super. We must have a swim later, Uel.' They could see for miles over the countryside.

'You are not wrong there, dearest,' replied Uel, her husband, and they hugged. 'We'll have to get that broken windowpane fixed soon though. I'll open the window now to air the place, shall I?'

'Yes do, dear. I'll give them a good clean, later.' She moved to the bathroom door. 'And just look at the bathroom! Just look at the size of the bath! It's enormous! You could bath an elephant, and still have room for a hippo,' Mary cried. Her voice echoed in the cavernous high-ceilinged room. 'They didn't scrimp on space in those days.'

'Are you saying I'm like a hippo?' Uel joked.

'Are you saying I'm like an elephant, Uel Middleton?' Mary frowned good-naturedly.

'Oh, of course not, Dearest. The thought never crossed my mind,' Uel grinned. *Well, only for a second,* he thought.

After an hour all had found rooms and carried their belongings indoors.

'Right people, we need to get things organised,' said Charlie in his normal voice. 'Take all the grub to the kitchen down that corridor. Sadie will show you where. Those as can cook can pitch in. Mr Wu will be in charge. He can do wonders with a bit o' chicken. I've eaten enough of it, so I should know.

'Me, Alex, George and Benny will find the boiler, if there is one, and get a fire going if possible. It is probably in the basement. I hope there is some fuel.' Charlie looked at the pile of equipment in the hall. 'The rest of you shift all this stuff upstairs, or to the kitchen or the drawing-room. Some of you can remove the dust covers from what furniture is left.'

'Wow, I have never been in an actual drawing-room before!' said Edith Higginson.

'Are there crayons an' pencils an' stuff?' asked Mary the Whittingtons' eldest.

'It's not that sort of drawing, Darling,' said Daphne, her mother. 'It's a kind of posh sitting room.'

'Tomorrow morning, we will elect a committee, so I am not ordering everyone about!' Charlie continued with a laugh. Everyone laughed too.

'You're doing a good job of it at the moment, Charlie,' said Daisy. Everyone laughed and set about their tasks.

The boiler, when they found it, was reasonably modern and was heated by a large wood-burning stove. A small heap of wood had fortunately been left in a corner.

'We'll have to chop some more wood first thing tomorrow,' said Benny Porter in his Staffordshire accent.

'Aye, this lot won't last long, so it won't,' added George McNeil in his Belfast accent.

All the men helped rake out the stove's ash and got a fire started. The boiler began to gurgle after a few minutes, and after the clanging of a few pipes, it seemed to settle down. Charlie felt the water tank after ten minutes. 'Yep, it's warming up nicely. The ladies will be able to wash the dishes,' he joked.

'Don't let "She-who-must-be-obeyed" hear you saying that,' laughed George.

'Don't let "She-who-must-be-obeyed" hear you saying what, George McNeil?' Daisy's sharp voice made them all turn. She stood with fists on hips and a glowering face. She was trying hard to look offended and not to smile.

'Erm, nothing, your Duchessness,' murmured George sheepishly, and making an extravagant bow like he had seen in films.

'I was just saying how wonderful you are, my Sweet,' Charlie said, trying to save the situation.

'Hmm, I don't believe a word of it. Come upstairs the lot of you, your tea's ready,' Daisy said, with mock sternness.

A great feast was spread on a table and was soon devoured: assorted sandwiches, sausage rolls and lots of sausages, with HP sauce.

'This will keep us going,' said Daisy.

'Thank you for that lovely grub ladies and Mr Wu,' said Charlie. Everyone agreed and applauded.

'Please to call Lee. Not Mistah Wu. Mistah Wu my dad,' said Lee Wu, smiling. 'We here are all friends.'

'Yes, certainly, Lee,' said Charlie smiling. 'Right, if everyone has their beds sorted, we can go outside to the terrace.'

'Ooo, "the terrace". Very la-dee-dah,' Sadie joked, pretending to fan herself like a posh lady and, throwing her head back, she sashayed outside.

'What else do I call it?' said Charlie laughing. 'We can enjoy the evening, without a view of the former gasworks and the smell from the sewage works!' All laughed again, and grabbing some chairs, followed Sadie out onto the terrace on the west side of the mansion. There was a glorious, rosy sunset sky above the treetops. The air was balmy and scented with blossoms.

'This is so lovely and ever so peaceful,' said Barbara Lyttle. 'I could sit here forever.'

'Yes, isn't it just. Lovely countryside, fresh air, and peace and quiet. What more could you ask for?' added Gwen Porter.

Just then the silence was shattered as a jet fighter plane flew low overhead. Everyone jumped. The little ones began to cry.

'What a racket!' cried Daisy, covering her ears and shouting to make herself heard.

'That must be from the RAF Barton airfield,' Thomas Jameson shouted.

'Cor, can we go there tomorrow, Dad? Please!' pleaded his son Tommy.

'Yes, if we have time, Tommy,' his father replied.

'I don't see why not. Tomorrow or soon anyway,' Charlie said, 'if we get everything done what needs to be done to get settled in. But there is no rush… we are here forever.'

'Time you young uns were in bed. Off upstairs with you, the lot of you,' said Sadie, looking at her watch. 'And no larking about. I don't want to hear a peep when we go indoors.' *Some hope,* she thought smiling.

'Get up those apples and pears,' said Harry Dunlop who liked using Cockney rhyming slang. 'And clean your Hampstead Heaths, or my trouble and strife will sort you out,' he laughed. His wife glared at him.

'Trouble and strife indeed!' she laughed, 'I'll give you trouble and strife, Harry Dunlop.' Everyone laughed.

'Yes, clean your teeth,' added Sadie.

'Aw, do we have to go to bed?' the children chorused.

'Yes!' their parents replied in unison laughing.

'And no larking about, as Mum says,' said Charlie smiLing.

Well, shut my north and south, thought Fred, meaning mouth. *I was right. We should have stayed in London,* he thought. *Still, no one mentioned anything about not having pillow fights.* He chuckled.

Chapter 10
'Oh Dear, What Time Is It?'

Next morning, they were up early at cockcrow, literally. Mr Grimsdale's rooster, Roddy, (Mrs Grimsdale was a Rod Stewart fan,) on the neighbouring farm, let everyone within about a quarter of a mile, when the wind was right, know it was morning. It strutted around crowing loudly.

Mr Grimsdale was already up and about attending to the milking of his large herd of Jersey cows. He had six men and women working for him. Mrs Grimsdale looked after their two hundred hens, free-range, collecting the eggs and feeding the hungry beaks.

'Oh dear, what time is it?' groaned Daisy trying to focus her eyes on the clock.

'Too early! Much too early,' replied Charlie, stretching and yawning. 'I slept like a log though, I did. This bed is so comfy.'

'Must be the clean country air,' said Daisy.

'Yeah, must be,' Charlie replied. 'You can hear the birds singing instead of coughing!' They both laughed. The dawn chorus was in full swing.

All the folk, summoned by the gong, soon gathered down in what was designated the dining room, as it was nearest to the kitchen. The smell of cooking made their mouths water. Lee Wu, his wife Brenda and some of the other women brought in plates of bacon, fried eggs, black pudding and toast, and pots of tea and coffee. Various boxes of cereal were available too.

Silence soon reigned as everyone tucked in. Even Fred was silent for once! After breakfast, Charlie said, 'That was delicious. Thank you to all who prepared it.

'Now, I want volunteers from you menfolk to wash-up before I pick you out!' Eventually, four men and Charlie put their hands up.

'We'll have to sort rotas for this sort of thing. Can't expect the same folk to do it every morning, and that includes you older kids!' Groans from the older kids. Fred looked horrified.

'Aw, Dad, do we have to?' moaned Fred. He was ignored. *Don't blame me if your bacon is burned and the toast is cremated!* he thought, craftily.

'When all's sorted, we will meet in the drawing-room and elect the committee,' Charlie continued. All agreed.

'You kids, make yourselves useful weeding the terrace while it is dry. It's a lovely day, out.

'Maybe we could take a drive over to the airfield later or tomorrow. I'll phone the commanding officer to see when's convenient. And there is an army barracks too, somewhere nearby I heard.' This was the headquarters of the two battalions of the Royal Bartonshire Light Infantry once commanded by the late Colonel Harry Harris mentioned earlier.

'Ooo, super,' said Fred, brightening up. *This place might not be so bad after all.*

When the adults had all gathered together, the children having been sent outside, but warned not to go near the lake, Charlie stood up.

'Right, first item on the agenda, rotas for cooking, washing-up, wood-chopping,' said Charlie. 'Who could draw them up?'

'I can do that,' said Carol Dunlop.

'Excellent. Thanks, Carol. Second item: election of committee,' Charlie continued. 'Oh! We need a secretary to write all this down. My bad,' Charlie said, slapping his wrist dramatically.

'I propose Gwen Porter,' said Thomas Jameson.

'Seconded,' said Benny Porter. Gwen glared in pretended annoyance at him but grabbed a pen and a notebook and began writing to catch up.

'I propose we have seven on the committee, with a quorum of five required for a vote,' said George McNeil. He had served on committees before for his former football club and darts team.

'I second that,' said Johnny Anderson.'

'Right, I think if each of us write seven names on pieces of paper, and the seven with the most votes will be our committeemen… erm… committee people, or persons,' Charlie said. 'And you cannot vote for yourself,' he laughed.

And so, for some minutes, everyone busied themselves thinking of names. Silence reigned. Many pencils were chewed.

The votes were then counted by Carol Dunlop and Annie McNeil.

'Right, we have a result,' Carol declared after some time counting and recounting. 'We have elected: Gwen, Alexander, my dear hubby Harry, Thomas, Sadie, Charlie, and Carol... Oh, that's me. And no, I didn't vote for myself,' she laughed.

'Right then, us seven can continue and the rest can go and check the building to see what needs doing by way of urgent repairs,' Charlie said. The others departed. Some were pleased they had not been elected.

'I propose Charlie be the chairman,' said Harry Dunlop.

'Seconded,' said Thomas Jameson.

'Okay, as duly elected chairman, the next item on the agenda is money,' said Charlie. 'In other words, how much do we have?'

'Erm, not a lot, Mr Chairman. The total is one hundred and fifteen thousand, six hundred and one pounds and a few pence,' said Sadie, who had noted every family's contribution. Each family had received "share certificates" in line with what they had contributed. £10 = one share. Mr Wu had contributed his compensation money which made up the bulk of the finances.

'Hmm, that won't last long with everyone to feed, and repairs needing doing,' Charlie said.

'I propose Sadie continues as treasurer and Carol as her assistant,' said Alexander Higginson.

'Seconded,' said Harry.

'Thank you, I think!' said Sadie laughing. She had a loud laugh.

'Priority is money for food. Those that have stall goods can hire stalls in the market on Thursdays,' said Charlie, 'and in other local towns.'

'That should bring in some cash,' said Sadie.

'We can do as many repairs as possible that don't need expensive parts, unless they are really essential,' said Carol. 'The main thing is to make the building weatherproof.'

'Yes, just repair windows in the rooms we're using and the chimneys too,' said Charlie. 'We can do the rest gradually. Just make sure they are weatherproof for now. And bird-proof. I noticed pigeons had got into some rooms and made a mess.'

'Okay, I'll get on to the British Heritage people, and what-ever government departments might do grants,' said Gwen. 'Bound to be some money looking for a worthy home.'

'The Agriculture Department maybe. We could get a grant for the land to plant something,' said Sadie.

'How about Christmas trees? They will be worth a packet come Christmas,' suggested Thomas.

'And we could raise turkeys. Lots of money in turkeys come Christmas,' added Carol.

'That's some ideas for long term, but we need something to bring in cash sooner,' Charlie said.

'Fishing! There's bound to be fish in that lake,' said Sadie. 'We could grant a daily licence to fish. Spread the rumour of a giant pike or trout called "The Major" or something. That'll reel in the punters.'

'And if there are not enough fish, we can… erm… borrow a few from the Thames which isn't far away,' said Harry.

'And Daisy and I will get our best gear on and go to see a bank manager about a mortgage. It is the only way we can get loads of cash quickly,' Charlie said.

'We should get oil or gas heating installed,' said Harry Dunlop. 'We don't have enough trees to last for long. We had better not chop them all down! There would be environment protesters chaining themselves to trees all over the place.'

'Good point, Harry. We shall keep that in mind, possibly before the winter. Right, that is enough to be going on with unless there is any more business.' Charlie waited a moment, but no one spoke. 'Meeting adjourned,' he declared, and he rapped the table with his knuckles. He was enjoying himself. *That went very well,* he thought.

Chapter 11
'Your New Committee Has Decided a Few Things'

When the committee emerged from the drawing room, most of the folk were standing around. Some of the men had headed off into the trees to saw up a few fallen branches.

'Right, everyone,' Charlie began. 'Your duly elected committee has decided a few important things.' Some smiles from the people. 'Those who have trade skills, check the state of the roof and chimneys. Check out the electrics to make sure they are safe. It could be years since they were last checked. A couple of the ladies round up the kids tomorrow morning and get them enrolled in the schools; it is only a few weeks till the end of term, but best to get them started. Most of them are primary school age. Take a couple of the vans.

'The rest start into window cleaning, stripping that old wallpaper an' any other stuff that needs doing. Just about everything needs cleaned.

'I an' the Duchess are off to see the bank manager!'

Everyone grinned and went off to their tasks. Soon, the sound of hard work could be heard. A voice started singing,

♪*Hi ho, hi ho, it's off to work we go! We work all day and get no pay…!* ♪ They all laughed and joined in.

Next day, Mildred Jameson and Daphne Whittington ferried the children into the town schools. The three oldest were introduced to the head-teacher of Market Barton Comprehensive, Mr Myles Smiley… he lived up to his name as he was a naturally good-natured type, unlike most head-teachers. The other twelve school-aged kids arrived at Samuel Street Primary, which was a dull red-brick Victorian edifice, but the staff were all very pleasant. Mildred enquired about a part-time teaching job and was asked to send a CV as there was a vacancy coming up next term. She was thrilled.

Quentin Lyttle and George McNeil, when they finished cutting firewood, began cutting panes of glass that had been brought with them, to make the windows of the rooms in use more weatherproof. The smell of putty soon wafted around.

'That should make the rooms a bit comfier,' commented Daisy. 'Keep the pigeons out at least. Nasty, feathered pests.'

Alexander Higginson, the plumber, began a thorough inspection of the pipework and water-tank. Benny Porter and Dante Whittington made their way to the roof to see what's what as regards repairs. There was a great deal which needed doing: loose slates, broken chimney pots, and blocked guttering, and worse, some guttering missing!

'Oh, that will cause damp,' said Dante. 'It will need fixing immediately. Just as well the roof wasn't lead-covered, or it would have all been nicked.'

'True. Hmm, we will need scaffolding to reach some of that guttering,' Benny said.

'That'll cost a few quid,' Dante observed. 'But needs must… safety first. Perhaps we could get a discount if we let the hire firm advertise that they are supplying the stuff?'

After supper, everyone reported on the day's events.

Mildred Jameson and Daphne Whittington said that the fifteen school-aged children had all been allocated to classes in the schools.

Mildred said, 'We will have to provide uniforms for the next term. As there are only a few days to go this term, both of the head-teachers said they will be okay until then.'

The local children were curious about what it was like to live in a real "castle". All the kids seemed to have made friends quickly and were happy. Well, as happy as a schoolkid can be.

Next day, when the children returned from their schools, they were taken in two vans to the RAF airbase and museum. Charlie put on his best duke-like impression at the barrier and asked to see the chap in charge as they were expected. The guard phoned the base commander's office and moments later, directed Charlie to the main offices, then he raised the barrier. The kids were totally excited.

Charlie and Quentin Lyttle drove to where the man indicated and, warning the children to stay put, they went into the building.

'Ah, Your Grace, how nice tae meet you. Ah'm Group Captain Hamish McSporran,' the base commander, who had a thick thatch of red hair, said as he rose from behind his desk and shook hands. He was a tall distinguished-looking man who spoke with a distinct Scottish accent. Charlie almost expected him to be wearing a kilt.

'Likewise,' Charlie said. 'Call me Charlie. No need for all this title malarkey. I'll come straight to the point, as I am sure you are busy, Hamish.' The group captain was glad none of his men were within earshot. He was not used to being addressed by his first name. 'As I explained on the phone, we have just moved into the mansion at Barton Hall, some forty of us,' Charlie continued, 'and the kids are keen to get a look at your planes, if that is no bother?'

'Aye, certainly, Charlie. Nae bother at all. Ah'll get one o' ma officers tae show them aroond. It will ha'e tae be quick though, as some will be takin' off for a routine patrol. Can't say where to... top secret! All very hush-hush,' McSporran chuckled and tapped the side of his nose. 'But they could always return some other day.'

'The Russians I suppose,' said Charlie. The officer only raised an eyebrow. 'That will be fine. It is good of you to let us in at such short notice, and of course, we can arrange another visit. It is just that they saw one of your planes fly over a few days ago, and they were so keen,' said Charlie.

'Aye, they make routine flights most days. But they will be avoiding your house fra' now on. Ah'll just get someone.' McSporran opened the door and asked his secretary to find Pilot Officer Susan Derwent.

The Pilot Officer arrived a few minutes later and saluted smartly. Charlie, Quentin and McSporran had gone outside.

'Ah, Pilot Officer Derwent, let me introduce Charlie Beaumont, tha new Duke. Could you show tha Duke and his children around some of tha planes? We ha'e about fifty minutes before they take-off,' McSporran said. 'They can then ha'e a look aroond tha museum for as long as they wish.'

'Yes, sir, be a pleasure,' she replied.

'Erm, they're not all mine, the kids,' Charlie chuckled. The two officers laughed when they saw all the children lined up. They had arranged themselves, under Fred's instruction, "tallest to the right, shortest to the left" and were like a flight of stairs.

'Come this way, Your Grace,' Officer Derwent said, and she saluted McSporran.

'Call me Charlie,' said Charlie, and he beckoned to the kids to join them.

Fred ordered, 'Right turn. Quick march!' And all the children marched, more or less in step, after the adults. A few little ones were not sure about right and left.

The children really enjoyed seeing the planes and speaking with some of the pilots.

'I'm going to be a fighter pilot when I grow up,' said Darren Middleton firmly.

'Me too,' added Mary Whittington, and several others.

All the kids returned home as happy as sandboys.

Chapter 12
The Mortgage

Next day, there was now a good-sized pile of wood in the basement to provide hot water, so the rest of the men and women took buckets of hot soapy water and began washing down the huge carved marble fireplaces, paintwork and walls. Accumulated dust from decades was removed. The late duke had paid off the servants.

Floors were brushed and hoovered thoroughly. Mary Middleton and a couple of others began cleaning and polishing the intricately carved wooden staircase banister, which was an immense task. But the glow of the mahogany soon returned. Then the tiled floor in the entrance was scrubbed and looked like new. Loose tiles were repaired.

'Makes you wonder what all those servants did, the state of this place! People will have to use a side door from now on, to keep this place clean,' said Mary Middleton, as she stood back, hands on hips to admire the result. 'It will be easier to get keys made for a side door, too.'

'The servants were all sacked,' said Sadie.

Olivia Anderson began producing pottery and paintings, local landscapes, for sale in the market, as did Edith Higginson with her knitted baby clothes. She began to sing quietly as she worked, ♫*Speed bonnie boat like a bird on the wing, Onward the sailor's cry. Carry the lad that's born to be king, Over the sea to Skye.* ♫ It was soon taken up by others working nearby. Then someone, a tenor, began to sing, ♫*Abide with me! Fast falls the eventide. The darkness deepens, Lord, with me abide!* ♫ They all smiled at one another and joined in enjoying the moment.

'We could start a choir,' Olivia commented. 'You do sound terrific!'

'Couldn't be any worse than some I've heard on TV,' said Daisy.

Carol produced the rotas for cooking and other tasks, and everyone stopped for a cup of tea, well-earned. Daphne, Barbara, Lee and Uel were down for cooking today's lunch, so when work recommenced, they departed for the kitchen.

It was decided that it was best to be selective about felling trees for wood. Some were obviously dead and should keep them supplied for some months, but oil or gas would be better in the future, so they began to investigate the relative costs.

Everyone with goods for sale would head to the local market on Thursdays. They hoped there would be no resentment from locals. Two of the men scouted around other towns to see what stalls might be needed.

'The missus and me, erm, and I, got a good result from the bank manager. They had held the deeds of the Hall before the last duke kicked the bucket, so he was willing to mortgage the place for two and a half million quid. Interest rate is pretty rough though,' Charlie said.

Everyone looked pleased, but apprehensive.

Daisy continued, 'However, we will all, that is all adult shareholders, have to sign up as jointly responsible. It would not be fair if "this enterprise", as the manager called it, went pear-shaped and one or two of us were left in the lurch.'

'That sounds reasonable,' said Carol Dunlop. All the others murmured agreement. 'It will make us all work the harder to make it a success.

'I had a phone call this afternoon,' she continued, 'from the British Heritage people. A man is coming tomorrow to speak about it, with the view of giving us a grant, provided we stick to their rules.'

'That sounds good,' Sadie said.

Charlie said, 'I'm heading over to see Mr Grimsdale at the farm in the morning. If he is willing, we could let him graze his cows on the lawn to get the grass down to a reasonable length, in exchange for milk or eggs and stuff.'

'Good idea,' said Lee Wu. 'Good fresh food, it make everyone much healthy. Tasty too.'

Chapter 13
'Just Call Me Charlie'

So, next morning, Charlie headed over to Harry Grimsdale's farm. As usual, Harry was fully occupied.

'Good morning, Harry,' Charlie shouted as he approached the milking parlour, which was very modern and efficient looking. Scores of cows were plodding into their slots on a large revolving platform ready to be connected to a milking machine. By the time the platform had rotated 360 degrees, the milking was completed, and the milking machine was removed. The cows then wandered off back to a field.

'Oh!' Harry looked up. 'It be yourself, Your Grace,' he said.

'Just call me Charlie, Harry. None of that title stuff, please,' Charlie said.

'Okay. What can I be doing for you, Charlie?' Harry asked.

'First, I would like to apologise for my mother's firing you as our caretaker. She tends to be abrupt, to put it mildly,' said Charlie.

'Think nothing of it. Mothers are all the same,' said Harry, and he laughed. 'You should hear my mother-in-law! Wowee! She would scare the pants off a banshee.'

'Tell me about it! I have one too. Fortunately, she stayed in London. Don't tell the missus I said that.' Charlie grinned and continued, 'Now, you know that big patch of long grass that was once a lawn?'

'Yeah, I know it,' said Harry.

'Well, there must be at least an acre or more, not that I, being a townie, know much about it, so could you use it for grazing in exchange for a supply of milk and stuff? Once that grass is eaten, we could let you have grazing on some of our other land… a few dozen acres… with reduced rent for a similar arrangement,' Charlie suggested. 'It isn't doing much at present.'

'Well, that sounds rather good. There be around an acre and a half in that there lawn. I can always use a bit o' grass for my Jerseys. Best milk you ever tasted is Jersey cow milk! The missus looks after the egg side of the farm, and a bit o' butter and cheese we make. How much milk you be needing?' Harry asked.

'Well, we have about forty-two folk altogether, including the children, so we will need lots of milk an' eggs and such,' Charlie said. 'Lots of growing kids… they eat us out of house and home.'

'Hmm, shouldn't be a problem. Might be better if I cut the lawn for silage though. No cow-pats all over it,' Harry laughed. 'The weather be exactly right for silage-making.' He looked up at the sky with an air of knowing. Even a townie like Charlie could tell it was hot and dry! 'Silage be best for cows in my opinion,' Harry added. 'None of that hay for my girls if I can help it.' He laughed.

'That sounds even better,' Charlie said.

'Then it's a deal. We can work out the details later. Let's shake on it,' Harry said. They shook hands and Charlie was given a glass of fresh milk.

'Wow! Delicious. You are right… it is the best.'

Chapter 14
'We Have Made Eight Hundred and Forty Pounds'

Back at the Hall, Charlie reported what had transpired at the farm.

'Sounds like a good arrangement. It will always be a steady income,' said Alexander Higginson. The rest agreed.

On Thursday evening, after the market, all the stallholders returned and reported having a successful day.

'The local people with stalls were a bit distant at first, but as our stalls don't really compete with theirs and a lot more people were attracted to the market, they soon became more friendly,' said Edith Higginson. 'There are no fish stalls, Charlie, so you should be okay there.'

Charlie nodded, 'I'll give it a go next week.'

'We have made a good sum: eight hundred and forty pounds altogether. Of course, we will need to buy in supplies for next market day,' said Mary Middleton.

'The markets in the other towns look good too,' said one of the men who had scouted them.

'Well, it all helps. The more markets we can cover the better,' said Charlie. 'I'll have to get my fish stall up and running. I could nip down to London real early to get fish and be back in time, hopefully, with that new stretch of motorway just completed from here to the M25 west of London.

'Now, it's time to eat,' and he rang the gong in the hall. A crowd appeared as if by magic!

Next day, two men from the British Heritage Trust arrived, Mr Brown and Mr Smith. No first names were offered. The committee members met them, and they had tea on the terrace.

'Am I correct in saying, Your Grace, that all these folk are a group of volunteers seeking to repair the building?' said the first man, Mr Brown.

'Yes, but please do call me Charlie. We are all friends come from London to establish this place as our home; me and the missus couldn't manage it on our own,' said Charlie, who being the Duke, thought it best to take the lead.

'Hmm, now, as a charitable organisation, we are willing to make a grant towards restoring and maintaining historical buildings and monuments, as you know. We, of course, must be careful as to where our supporters' money goes. Every pound must be accounted for. I understand Barton Hall is a Grade One listed building,' Mr Brown said.

'Yes, it certainly is but as you can see, there are a few bits as need doing,' Charlie said. He pointed to a pile of debris carefully collected.

'Yes, quite so. Strict rules must be applied, however. All restoration work must be in accordance with the original. For example, these bits of stonework from the roof parapet. They can be reused where possible or replacements carved using the same source of stone,' Mr Brown said.

'And the chimney pots,' said the second man Mr Smith. 'You will be required to reproduce items in keeping with the original.'

'We have a lady who does pottery,' said Sadie.

'Excellent. Now, we must have a look inside of course,' said Mr Brown.

'Yes, certainly, if you have finished your tea, we can go indoors,' said Sadie. She was in her element entertaining folk.

'Yes, and a delicious tea it was, too,' said Mr Smith dabbing the corners of his mouth with a napkin. The napkins had all been embroidered with the Coat of Arms by Edith Higginson and some of the older girls. Sadie beamed with pleasure. She was so proud of her tea making. She had prepared dainty sandwiches with the crusts removed for the occasion. Charlie thought they were a bit too dainty for his liking: he could have eaten four at a time! But Sadie had warned everyone, especially her son and grandson, to behave mannerly. 'Do not be showing us up, Charlie,' she ordered. Fred was watched with an eagle eye. He was the model child, for once.

'Hmm, you have removed some wallpaper already, I see,' Mr Brown said when they entered the hallway. He looked very displeased.

'Yes, some of it was peeling off and was looking rather dirty and untidy,' said Carol.

'Yes, well, I suppose that is alright, as long as it is replaced with similar quality and period design,' said Mr Smith.

'Erm… we were just going to paint it,' said Charlie innocently. The two men looked horrified.

'Oh no, no, that will never do at all, Mr Beaumont...
erm... Charlie. That won't do at all! Not if the original was
wallpaper. No, that won't do at all,' said Mr Brown.

'We don't have the cash to afford posh wallpaper for all
these rooms. We are just making ends meet as it is,' said
Sadie.

'Well, perhaps we can assist you there,' said Mr Smith.

Mr Brown said, 'We will get our experts to design suitable
replacements for the main rooms; do keep some samples and
we will pay for the printing. Even better, perhaps we could
take some samples with us and do some measurements of the
rooms while we are here, if we may?' Charlie enthusiastically
nodded agreement. 'You may paint the minor rooms, bedrooms and such, tastefully of course, if you wish. Stay with
the original colours where possible. The eighteenth century
had certain colours which were in fashion. Here are some
samples of suitable colours.' He handed over a colour chart.
'No structural changes may be made without consulting us
first, of course.' Mr Smith nodded in agreement.

'We can handle that, no problem,' said Charlie.

'What about the gate lodge? Can we knock it down?'
asked Sadie. 'It is almost down already.'

'Hmm. It is a much later addition, or probably a replace-
ment in Victorian times. All country estates had a gate lodge.
One couldn't expect the gentry to open their own gates,
what?' said Mr Brown. He almost smiled. Everyone chuckled.
'It is of little historical value I'm afraid, but it might be best
to retain it. It would enhance the entrance. Perhaps you might
wish to employ a gatekeeper?'

'We will hardly need one,' said Sadie. *Waste of money,*
she was thinking.

'Okay, we'll think about what to do with it,' Charlie said, 'and let you know before we do anything.'

When the men had finished measuring the rooms and estimating the quantities of paper required, Charlie, Daisy and Sadie shook hands with them, and they departed. Everyone breathed a sigh of relief.

Next morning, everyone gathered round after breakfast to hear the updated situation.

Gwen read them out. 'First, we are going to get a grant for new posh wallpaper in the main rooms. Once the walls are stripped of the old stuff, we could possibly paint them in the meantime, as it will be months before new paper is ready.

'Second, we could knock down the old gate lodge. Benny and Harry, see what stone you could salvage if we do so. It might do to replace the broken bits on the roof; also, the chimney pots if they match the ones on the house. Olivia, can you make some if necessary?'

'Yes, certainly,' Olivia Anderson replied. 'No problem, if my kiln is big enough. I'll need to see one up close.'

'Third, as the weather is forecast dry today, we can spruce up the outside as much as possible. The children can continue weeding the steps and terrace.' The children were not so keen.

'Fourth, Mr Grimsdale is willing to rent some land for silage-making and grazing for his cows. He is going to start with our, erm, lawn.' Some laughter. 'He will also supply milk and eggs in part exchange.'

'Last, we have got a mortgage from the bank. Mr Freeburn, the manager, is coming today for us all to sign up for it. We mentioned this before, so stay close to the Hall.'

'Thank you, Gwen,' Charlie said. 'Any questions?' There was a thoughtful silence. 'Right, though we have the possibility of some cash, we must not be wasteful. Switch off lights and things when not in use for example. Parents make sure your kids don't go leaving lights on or taps running. Do you hear that, Freddie?'

Fred scowled. *Why pick on me?* He thought. *I always turn the lights off. Well, most of the time.*

'There is a lot to do but if we all pull together, we can do it! One for all, and all for one!' Charlie concluded. A lot of applause at this and they all cried, 'One for all, and all for one!'

'Can I suggest we start opening a few rooms for bed and breakfast as soon as possible?' said Daphne Whittington, 'Once we get sorted of course. Posh folk will pay a lot to stay in a place like this, I'm sure.'

'Yes, that sounds a good idea. We can set up a website. Their rooms, breakfast room an' that, would have to be kept separated from our lot. Can't have a mob of kids annoying paying guests,' said Sadie. 'Keys for the front door could be a problem as they are so big and clumsy. We will have to get them to use a smaller side door, with a modern lock so they can come and go. The one on the west terrace will be best as it is nearest the carpark. I asked Mr Smith about that, and he agreed it will be okay.' Everybody agreed.

And so, everyone set about the day's tasks with a spring in their steps.

Chapter 15
It Seemed Like a Hundred Years' Worth of Dust Flew Into the Air

Gradually, the immediate tasks were completed. All the rooms in use had had the window glass mended, window sashcords checked and replaced where necessary, which meant most of them; roof slates and chimney pots repaired, and bedrooms painted. The electric wiring was found to be in good condition but might need replacing in a few years. The main reception rooms still awaited the new wallpaper that was being hand-printed by a specialist firm.

All the carpets had been rolled up and carried outside, by several men, to the terrace and given a good beating. The children enjoyed doing this! It seemed like a hundred years' worth, or more, of dust, flew into the air. They were then shampooed. This took a lot of time.

Some areas of carpet were a bit worn, so it was decided when the carpet was back *in situ* the worn bits would be hidden with furniture where possible or placed in less walked-on areas.

'I wonder what all those servants did. These carpets, in fact, the whole house, haven't been given a good seeing to in years,' Daisy commented.

'There probably has been a shortage of servants for years, especially if the last duke had lost all his money and sacked many,' Sadie said.

'Yeah, you are probably right, Sadie,' Daisy replied.

Meanwhile, Carol Dunlop, the retired teacher, and Mildred Jameson were working on a website for a bed and breakfast. It was hoped to take in their first paying guests the following spring.

Mildred had also obtained a teaching place in the primary school in the city.

The large ground floor rooms at the front of the mansion had been converted into bedrooms with *en suite* bathrooms. Some four-poster beds from upstairs, brought back to their original condition as near as possible, were installed in the guest rooms. More than a few mattresses had to be replaced. Some of the ladies had purchased suitable decoration in the form of material for curtains, statuettes and paintings, when they could be obtained cheaply in auctions or salvage yards. Large paintings were unsuitable for most modern homes, so, were usually bought at a reasonable price. Olivia turned her hand to restoring them and regilding the frames. Initially in total eight rooms offered a high degree of Georgian/modern luxury. This would be reflected in the price charged for an overnight stay.

A smaller reception room was designated as the breakfast room for guests. It had a degree of privacy from the other inhabitants, though curious children often had to be shooed away.

Daphne Whittington got a few nursing shifts at the city hospital. Some of the other women took turns to look after the two pre-school children. New arrivals were expected in a few months! The Hall's population was growing.

At the next committee meeting it was reported that with the income from market stalls in five local towns, and other employment, their finances were looking healthier, along with the land rent from Mr Grimsdale. He found this arrangement very satisfactory.

The Department of Agriculture had paid over a grant for planting trees. Six thousand fir and spruce trees had been purchased and were delivered in batches. The men were busy planting several acres of them mainly around the lake. Allowing for some casualties, it was reckoned in a year or two these Christmas trees would bring in a good profit. Continual replacements would ensure a steady harvest. Native deciduous trees were also planted to replace dead ones along the driveway.

It was decided eventually to rebuild part of the gate-lodge so that guests and anglers would not have to open and close the gates themselves. It also made it possible for someone to collect fees from anglers. It had been decided that a limited number of people would be allowed in to fish the lake each day to conserve stocks, therefore there was a rota in place for gate duty from seven a.m. until dusk during the angling season. Many local angling enthusiasts were quickly lured and hooked.

The lake had been found to have a good stock of brown trout and some pike. Some baby fish were also regularly raised in tanks housed in the old stables. Harry Dunlop and Johnny Anderson oversaw this operation.

Prior to the angling season commencing, the existence of "a giant pike" had been hinted at in local pubs.

Charlie told the assembled Hall folk that the next operation was to tidy up the long driveway. The next Saturday, which was a dry day, everyone possible was out weeding the gravel and repairing potholes. The older children wheeled the pile of weeds to a compost heap in the old walled garden. Nothing went to waste. Harry Dunlop and helpers had dug this over and planted vegetables, which in time saved a large food bill, and some flowers were grown with which to decorate the guest bedrooms during the holiday season.

When all the driveway had been cleared, a small army with rakes levelled the gravel and left all looking neat.

'Very nice, very nice indeed! Looks proper grand, it does!' someone declared. They were all extremely pleased.

Mr Grimsdale had taken his crop of silage from the large lawn, and now it was beginning to resemble what it was described as.

The committee released funds for a large motor-mower which kept the lawn looking presentable. The older children loved using this. In the end, the driver was selected by drawing lots to stop the arguing. Some arguments had come to blows!

Chapter 16
Some Unexpected Visitors!

Then, one day, about six months later, out of the blue came a bombshell which threatened to destroy all their work.

A vintage silver Rolls Royce drove up and parked in front of the house. Mr Augustus Grimm senior and his two partners descended, briefcases in hand. They looked serious, grim, greatly perturbed. This was obviously not a social visit.

Charlie was called to meet them urgently. He had been up on the roof mending a chimney.

'Hey, you guys, what brings you here?' Charlie said cheerfully.

Mr Grimm senior cleared his throat and said, 'Your Grace,' no informality for Mr Grimm senior, 'I am afraid I have some troubling news for you. May we talk somewhere privately?'

'You can say what you have to say in front of us all, Mr Grimm,' Charlie said. He was feeling worried, and so did the folk who had gathered round. They sat down on some garden chairs reclaimed from salvage and lovingly restored.

'Very well. I have just received a communication from the representatives of a certain person by the name of Montague Beaumont,' said Mr Grimm taking a folder from his briefcase.

'Never heard of him,' said Charlie.

'Me neither,' said Sadie.

'That's as may be, but this person, Montague Beaumont, is putting himself forward as a claimant to the title of Duke of Bartonshire,' Mr Grimm senior said.

Everyone was dumbfounded. Even Sadie was speechless, for once!

'He can't do that!' cried Sadie when she recovered. 'We have slogged our guts out getting this place in order. Can he?' Everyone looked anxiously at Mr Grimm senior.

'We are not giving it up, not without a fight,' cried Charlie.

'We were hoping you would say that Mr Beaumont,' said Mr Grimes.

'Yes indeed,' said Mr Grimm junior. 'We, therefore, propose to fight your case *pro bono…*'

'Pro what?' Charlie asked.

'*Pro bono*. It means free of charge, Your Grace,' said Mr Grimm senior. 'As our firm, to our regret, seems to have missed this person in our research, we will fight it all the way.'

'In court, you mean?' asked Daisy.

'Yes, Mrs Beaumont, in court, should it come to that. We are certain he is an imposter. He has declined a DNA test which is suspicious,' said Mr Grimes.

'Bring it on, dude, bring it on,' Charlie said thumping a fist into his other hand, and the others cheered.

'We'll show him,' said Sadie. She shook a fist at the world in general.

'Very good. We thought it best that you knew of the situation immediately. We shall leave you now and shall spend some days researching this person. We shall keep you informed of developments should they arise. Again, we are deeply sorry for this,' said Mr Grimm senior.

'No problem, Mr Grimm. We aren't beaten yet,' Charlie said. 'Far from it. We Beaumonts have never avoided a good scrap. I'm sure one of us was at Waterloo!'

'But you'll partake of some tea and freshly baked scones before you return to London?' Sadie said.

'That would be most acceptable. Thank you,' said Mr Grimm senior smiling. He rarely turned down a good brew or a scone.

Chapter 17
Montague Beaumont Makes
an Appearance

The Hall folk were still discussing recent events some hours later when another large car, a black Bentley, drove through the gates and stopped at the mansion. A chauffeur in livery put on his cap as he got out and opened a rear door for a well-dressed man to exit.

The man was aged about thirty-five, wore a dark blue Savile Row suit, crimson cravat with a diamond pin, and carried a silver-topped ebony cane.

'What a toff,' muttered Daisy. 'No way he is a Beaumont.'

'Prat more like,' said Sadie. 'No guessing who this is. That so-called relative of ours. I bet he is as fake as a nine-pound note.'

'Good afternoon,' he said with an upper-class accent as he reached the top of the steps. 'I wish to speak to Mr Charles Beaumont. Is he available?' He could see no one who resembled a duke in his opinion.

'I am Charles Beaumont, the Duke of Bartonshire. Who might you be?' Charlie replied, stepping forward. He looked at Montague as if he were a bad smell. He had guessed who this bloke was and had used his title for effect.

'I, my dear sir, am Montague Beaumont, the Duke of Bartonshire… the rightful Duke of Bartonshire.'

'Oh, no you aren't,' shouted Daisy. 'Charlie here is the Duke all legal and proper. So, sling yer hook, mister.' She looked menacing.

'I have no wish to bandy words with you people,' Montague replied snootily. 'You are trespassing on my estate, so I will give you one week to vacate these premises,' he said. He looked at each face in turn, sneering.

'It is you what is trespassing, whatever your name is. Get off my property now before my boot connects with your fake aristocratic behind!' Charlie stabbed a finger at Montague Beaumont's cravat. Charlie rarely lost his temper, but now he was restraining himself with difficulty from hitting Montague a thump on the nose.

'We shall see about that. My lawyers will be in touch,' Montague said, and turned to leave.

'Ah, I see you are using my cups and saucers… my property.' Montague lifted a cup with the Beaumont Coat of Arms on it that had been left on a garden table. 'If you damage any of my property, I shall sue you for every penny.' He replaced the cup on the table.

'Clear off, before we set the dogs on you!' shouted Daisy. Benny Porter's Rottweiler dogs Brutus and Sabre, stood nearby, looking hungry. Sabre licked his lips as if on cue. They were real softies to those who knew them. The children all loved them.

'On yer bike!' shouted Charlie. 'And take your fancy chauffeur with you.' The chauffeur was waiting patiently by the car.

'See you in court, you fake,' cried Sadie livid with rage.

Montague sniffed haughtily, 'You will be hearing from my lawyer.' He turned on his heel, descended the steps and got back into his car. The chauffeur closed the door, got in and it drove off scattering gravel as they went.

When Montague had gone, Charlie, in a moment of inspiration, lifted the cup carefully and put it in a paper bag.

'The cheek of that little pipsqueak coming here all airs and graces, trying to steal our inheritance,' said Charlie. 'He is no relative of mine I'm certain. I can tell.'

'After all our hard work! No way, José,' said Johnny Anderson. Everyone agreed.

'He'll get this place over my dead body,' declared Charlie. 'I'd burn it down first!' They all went indoors, and later, Sadie phoned the Grimms. She gave them time to have returned to London.

'Could I speak to either Mr Grimm or to Mr Grimes please?' she asked the receptionist.

'I will put you through to Mr Grimm junior who is available, Madam. Who may I say is calling?'

'Sadie Beaumont, that's who,' Sadie replied.

Presently Mr Grimm junior said, 'Ah, Mrs Beaumont, we were expecting a call. I assume you have met Montague Beaumont. His lawyers have just been in contact with us. They sounded surprised you did not believe Montague!'

'Yes, we have met him. It was all Charlie could do not to hit him, and if that stuffed shirt thinks he is getting his paws on this property, he has another think coming!' Sadie said angrily.

'I quite agree,' said Mr Grimm junior, smiling to himself. 'We have already hired a private detective to check on our Montague Beaumont. We are also going through his supposed claim to be the descendant of the second son of the Third Duke, who died in 1853 I believe.

'This second son, Reginald, fell out of favour with his father due to his profligate lifestyle. The Third Duke was quite shall we say, tight with his cash. Reginald and his wife Belle, a rather unpleasant French character by all accounts, were cut off without a penny, and one presumes that is why he does not appear on the family tree. Pruned one might say.' He had a little chuckle at his joke. Sadie could not help laughing.

'That sounds good. I hope your detective can dig up something,' said Sadie. 'How soon do you think you will hear anything, Mr Grimm?'

'One is unable to say, Mrs Beaumont, but very soon one hopes. We have already requested a court hearing at the Old Bailey,' Mr Grimm junior said.

'Good. Thank you very much, Mr Grimm. Goodbye.' Sadie hung up the phone and relayed the news to the people.

'We will just have to wait then,' Charlie said. 'Okay, guys, back to work. We are staying put. And I am going to pay the cops a little visit.'

Everyone cheered. At least now there was some hope of winning.

Chapter 18
The Court Case Commences

'Would the counsel for the plaintiff please present your case,' said the judge, Justice George Henry Carmichael, when the court finally sat. It was an unusual case, and the judge was relishing every moment.

Many of the Hall folk were in court, along with some reporters from upmarket newspapers and magazines. The dispute over the dukedom was of some interest to their readers. Many sided with the plaintiff Montague; few with "that fishmonger chap".

Mr Jeremiah Samson a law partner with Samson, Blackwall and Quigg, stood and began, 'My Lord, this is a case of an error of identity and of right by descent. My client, Mr Montague Beaumont, wishes to lodge his claim to be recognised as the rightful Duke of Bartonshire.

'Mr Beaumont was abroad, in the outback of Australia in fact, when the previous duke sadly perished along with his heirs and has just recently returned. It was only then he heard of the tragedy. I am sure Your Lordship is aware of the incident.' The judge nodded thoughtfully. He had, of course, read of the disaster which befell the late duke.

Samson continued, 'My client is the direct descendant of the second son, Reginald George Beaumont, of the Third Duke, Bernard George Beaumont.

'The person, the defendant, one Charles Beaumont, who was mistakenly awarded the title some months ago, has refused to vacate the family seat, namely Barton Hall, Bartonshire. He is descended, we are told, from the third or fourth son of the Third Duke, the number is of no consequence, one Thomas James Beaumont, so my client has a better claim... indeed the rightful claim.

'My client is not unmoved by the amount of work this person has done to renovate the property, and he is willing to offer financial compensation, in due course. My client, at present, finds himself somewhat low in funds.'

'He is after money!' Sadie muttered. 'Probably wants to sell the Hall.'

'"Not unmoved"! I'll move him with the toe of my boot,' Charlie muttered fairly loudly sitting next to Mr Grimm senior. Next to them were Messrs Grimm junior and Grimes.

'Silence! I will not tolerate interruption in my court,' the judge said. He looked at Charlie disdainfully.

Mr Samson continued, 'The person, Charles Beaumont's claim to be the true heir of the late duke is invalid, so My Lord, my client wishes only to gain what is rightfully his. Thank you.' He sat down.

'Mr Grimm, I understand you represent Mr Charles Beaumont. Is that correct?' asked the judge. He looked at Charlie over his spectacles.

Mr Grimm senior stood slowly. His back was playing him up. 'Yes, I have that pleasure, My Lord. My client was awarded the title, as my Learned Friend states, as he is the legitimate descendant of the Third Duke.

'I would like to put a few questions to Mr Montague Beaumont, with your permission, My Lord?'

'Very well. Mr Montague Beaumont, please come forward,' said the judge.

Montague Beaumont sat down in the witness box looking every inch the gentleman. He looked down his nose at Charlie and sniffed like there was a bad smell. Charlie glared at him.

'Mr Beaumont, you have stated in your claim that you are Montague George David Beaumont, the only son of David George Beaumont, deceased. For the sake of time, I shall not read all your claimed forebears, but you claim to be a direct descendant of the… who was it… the second son of the Third Duke, one Reginald George Beaumont,' said Mr Grimm senior.

'Yes, that is correct,' said Montague. 'I have researched my lineage and I am the only living male of that line.'

'Montague George David Beaumont attended Eton College some twenty or so years ago,' said Mr Grimm senior. 'Who was the headmaster then, Mr Beaumont?'

'Oh, it is so long ago. One cannot recall his name, I'm afraid,' said Montague waving a hand dismissively. 'One would rather forget one's school days. They were rather tiresome, what?' he laughed. No one else did.

'Then let me refresh your memory: it was Dr William Thackeray. It is strange you would forget such an esteemed individual, the headmaster of your *alma mater*! You did learn Latin did you not, Mr Beaumont?' Mr Grimm senior asked.

'Erm, yes, a little. I'm afraid what one learned has largely slipped one's memory. It was never my best subject,' said

Montague. He was hoping Mr Grimm would refrain from more Latin-based questions. In fact, he was getting rather worried. *Ut anxius,* in fact.

'You seem to have forgotten a lot, Mr Beaumont, but let us move on. Montague George David Beaumont then attended Oxford University where he read classical Greek literature and history,' said Mr Grimm. Montague started to get extremely worried. He could feel cold sweat trickle down his spine. His mouth went dry.

Mr Grimm continued, 'I shall not insult you by asking you to tell us some of this history. You may have forgotten it.' Some titters from the assembled Hall folk. Charlie grinned. 'Perhaps you could tell us when you left Oxford, and where you took up employment?'

'Erm, I left, let me think, thirteen years ago, and I went to work in the City, with a financial firm, J. J. Bloggs and Co.' Montague stated confidently. He was relieved to have avoided anything Greek and to get back to safer ground.

'Hmm, that is correct,' stated Mr Grimm senior. Montague breathed easier. 'However, I would point out a few discrepancies in your story, Mr Beaumont, if that be your real name.' The Hall folk were all ears, as was the judge. 'The headmaster in the real Montague George David Beaumont's time at Eton College was Dr William Thompson, not William Thackeray. He was a novelist of some renown, as any well-educated young man would know. Young Montague did indeed read Greek history at Oxford but was dismissed, "sent down" I believe the term is, after two years for failing in his studies. It seems he preferred to spend his evenings in the local bars with rather dubious… erm… ladies. No more questions, My Lord.' Some tittering from the Hall folk.

'You may step down, Mr Beaumont,' said the judge. Montague made a hasty retreat.

'I am not yet finished, My Lord, if you would be so kind as to indulge my line of questioning for a while longer,' said Mr Grimm senior. The Judge nodded. 'I call Mr Daniel Sol of Ross Bros, Gents' Outfitters, with your permission, My Lord?' The judge nodded again. He was intrigued, like everyone else in the room.

Daniel Sol, a handsome, well-dressed, neatly groomed, young gent aged about twenty-five, took the stand. He had a smile which rarely strayed from the corners of his mouth.

'Mr Sol, thank you for appearing as a witness. Do you recognise anyone in this courtroom?' Mr Grimm senior asked.

'Yes, I recognise that gentleman there.' He pointed at Montague.

'How do you know this person, Mr Sol?'

'He hired the suit that he is wearing some weeks ago. He should have returned it by now, in fact, several weeks ago!'

'Thank you, sir, you may step down,' said Mr Grimm senior.

'My Lord, I would call another witness with your permission?' said Mr Grimm. The judge nodded. Montague was really worried by now… sweating blood as they say.

'I call Mrs Janet Albertson of "Albertson's Luxury Car Hire" to the stand. Mrs Albertson entered the room and sat down. She was a very tall, thin lady with her grey hair pinned up in a bun at the back of her head.

'Mrs Albertson, do you recognise anyone in the courtroom?' asked Mr Grimm senior.

'Yes, I do,' she replied having looked around. She pointed at Montague. 'Him there.'

'How do you know that person?' asked Mr Grimm.

'He hired one of our cars and a chauffeur for a day. His cheque bounced and he gave a false address,' she added with a withering look at Montague.

'Thank you, Mrs Albertson. You may step down.

'With your permission, I call Mr Norbert Gregg, My Lord.' The judge nodded. He was intrigued by the proceedings.

'My detective friend Mr Norbert Gregg has done some research on my behalf. I will now ask him to take the stand,' said Mr Grimm. Montague was ready to make a hasty exit. Gregg was an ordinary-looking man in a brown coat, so he blended in with the crowd when tailing suspects.

'Mr Gregg, could you tell the good folk here, and His Lordship, what you have learned about this person who claims to be Montague Beaumont?'

Gregg looked at his notebook. 'This person was born in Bedford, the son of a tailor. He left school aged sixteen with no qualifications, though he apparently excelled in amateur dramatics.' He paused so that the fact lodged with his hearers. 'He has never been to Eton, or to any university that I could discover, and has rarely been employed for more than a few months, usually in unskilled work. At his last employment, he was fired for poor timekeeping according to the manager... he rarely bothered to turn up!' Some laughter from the Hall folk. Even the judge was amused. Reporters were writing furiously. 'Moreover, there is no record of a Montague Beaumont having travelled to Australia in recent years.'

Mr Grimm then asked, 'Have you ever been to Bedford, Mr Beaumont... I shall use the name in the meantime?' Montague said nothing but went red in the face. 'I believe you originate from 25, Riverside Street, Bedford as Mr Gregg has stated, the son of Bill and Sandra of that address. In fact, as far as attending university is concerned, have you ever even driven, in the Bentley and chauffeur you hired for a day, through the city of Oxford, as I am certain that is the closest you have come to a university?

'Have you ever been in prison for fraud, Mr Beaumont?' Again, Montague was silent. 'I would inform the court, My Lord, that the police have matched his fingerprints found on a cup he handled at Barton Hall, to Mr Oswald SMITHERS!' Mr Grimm senior paused for effect. 'Oswald Smithers, who has a criminal record as long as my arm!' An awed silence prevailed.

'Drink, that is the alcoholic variety, seems to have been the real Montague George David Beaumont's undoing, Mr Smithers, as he died five years ago from liver problems according to the forensic pathologist who did the autopsy! And is interred in the family plot in Highgate Cemetery, London!' Mr Grimm senior glared at Montague/Oswald. 'You look remarkedly well for a corpse, Mr Smithers!' The Hall folk were ecstatic, shaking each other's hands vigorously.

The judge sat open-mouthed for a few moments, and then called for order.

'Have you anything to say, Mr... erm... Smithers?' asked the judge. Smithers shook his head. The judge shook his head. 'Case dismissed. Officers, arrest this imposter!' Two burly police officers moved on a trembling Oswald and yanked him out of his seat.

Then pandemonium broke out. Newspaper reporters rushed to the phones, Mr Samson threw down his pen in defeat and disgust at how he had been deceived by Smithers. He saw no hope of payment for his services. He predicted that a cheque which Montague/Oswald had presented that morning would also "bounce".

Charlie and his friends jumped for joy and slapped Mr Grimm senior on the back. He chuckled for the first time in years. He felt twenty years younger than his… let us just say, he was getting on a bit.

The three lawyers joined the Hall folk in a celebration tea in the "Ritz", at Mr Grimm senior's expense. He had already booked some tables in advance, as he was confident that he would win the case. He had not had so much fun in decades. His colleagues could not believe the change in him.

'Wow, me in the Ritz! Who'd have thought it?' exclaimed Benny Porter looking around at the décor.

Chapter 19
A Well-Wisher
Contributed Generously

When the folk returned to Barton Hall that evening, there was another celebration. Even the little ones were permitted to stay up late.

Next day, everyone was tired but set about their tasks with happy hearts and new resolve.

All the trees had been planted, and two of the men manned the gate-lodge awaiting the first anglers. They were replaced every two hours as other Hall folk followed a rota.

On the first day, ten anglers turned up armed with rods, bait, all the paraphernalia the avid angler accumulated, and flasks of tea. They all reported a successful day and promised to tell their friends. Soon, a steady income fed the funds for some months during the fishing season.

The folk with trades advertised in the city and surrounding area, and soon built up work doing carpentry, glazing, window cleaning and chimney sweeping.

The promised new wallpaper arrived on schedule. Willing hands set about decorating the entrance hall in sky blue with gold fern leaves and flower pattern; the dining room in crimson with silver sprays of flower buds and tracery; the breakfast room-cum-television room for guests and the drawing room, in pale lilac and green with similar sprays of flowers in gold and silver. When finished, two weeks later, they stood back and admired their work. They took great satisfaction in the finished product. Careful measuring of each roll meant there was little wastage. They knew additional paper would have been expensive.

'We are looking like a real mansion, now,' commented Daisy. Everyone agreed. Lee Wu appeared with chilled champagne for all (adults only) and cream doughnuts for everyone. Fred, now aged ten, was not impressed! *The olds have all the fun, as usual,* he thought grumpily, but he tucked into the cream doughnuts provided. Most of the kids had faces covered in cream.

Next day, the men from British Heritage arrived and added their approval, plus a substantial cheque towards further renovations. A well-wisher, who wished to remain anonymous, had read of their efforts and contributed generously. She had been the wealthy victim of a burglary with violence, a few years earlier, by one Oswald Smithers, and she had read the court case story in the paper. Charlie requested that their gratitude be passed on.

The next committee meeting reported a healthy income. The mortgage repayments were being met, the number of guests was increasing, the bills for electricity, oil-fired central heating (newly installed), council tax etc. were also being paid. Solar panels discretely placed on the roof met most of their electric usage. Everyone was asked to think of more money-raising ideas.

'We could open up more ground floor rooms for guests. There are about another twenty suitable,' suggested Carol. 'They are not as large as the ones we are using, but they would appeal to some at a lower price per night.'

'I think we should make a start at repaying the mortgage sum. We don't want to leave it for our kids to be lumbered with it,' suggested Sadie.

'Yeah, the sooner we clear it the better; we will save on all the interest payments,' Harry Dunlop added.

'We promised the local folk a party when we first came here,' said Sadie.

'Yes, we should keep our promise,' Charlie said. 'We could maybe get a funfair or something to come and have games for the kids and a few "older" kids! And eatables… lots of eatables.' He licked his lips.

'Yeah, the lawn is big enough, now it actually looks like a lawn,' said Daisy. 'I have never lived in a house with a lawn before. Not even a window-box!'

'Me neither!' the rest said in unison. They all laughed.

And so, "Finn O'Flaherty's Funfair" was booked for the second Saturday the following month, and circulars were given out in the city and posters put up. Everyone hoped for a dry day.

The day before, stacks of loaves and sandwich fillings were bought, and early on the day, everyone was busy with preparations.

At ten a.m. the public began to arrive in carloads. A field was turned into a car park. Fortunately, the sun was shining. Two local brass bands took turns in providing music. Miss Molly McPherson's Scottish Dance Class put on a display.

The funfair was a great attraction and soon the place was hiving. Mr O'Flaherty was extremely pleased.

After lunch, the bands had a rest and everyone gathered for games: egg and spoon races, three-legged races, and five-a-side football. It was meant to be five-a-side but ended up with about twenty players in each team as many wanted to play: the Barton Hall United team versus Market Barton Rovers. It was all good-natured, and there were that many goals scored the referee lost count, so he declared a draw, and everyone cheered. Fred claimed he scored three.

'We'll beat you next time,' was a commonly heard remark, in jest of course.

When the last visiting folk had departed, Charlie and all the Hall people sat down and breathed a sigh of relief. 'That went very well I think,' he said.

'It was very much super,' said Lee Wu, who had spent the day cooking sweet and sour chicken. 'We make lots of "lolly" for funds,' he said. He was picking up slang quickly.

'Yes, everyone seemed to enjoy it,' said Sadie.

'Aye, they did too. We should make it an annual event maybe,' suggested Mildred Jameson.

'Yes, we definitely should,' said Charlie. 'But for now, let's just REST! I have never felt so tired. No more football for me! Not with my stomach!' He patted his large belly. They all laughed.

'Especially as you were sent off for diving to get a penalty,' added Daisy and everyone laughed again.

'I was not diving! I was fouled, I was. I should have got a penalty,' Charlie declared, not too convincingly.

'What a day!' declared Dante Whittington.

'Yep, it was,' said Olivia Anderson. 'But time for bed for the little ones.'

'Get up those apples and pears,' said Harry Dunlop using Cockney rhyming slang. Everyone laughed, and they all went indoors.

The next three years were tough going; the COVID 19 pandemic hit hard. The folk worked around the premises or did outside work when possible. They were careful to keep away from others in case the virus infected the Hall folk. When things returned to normal the old stables were hired out to "the horsey set" as Sadie called them and had become popular. A local blacksmith made regular visits to shoe the horses. The... erm... by-product of the horses was spread around the Christmas trees.

A large barn at the rear of the stables was now operating as a turkey farm, from the autumn until Christmas. Turkey chicks were bought from various breeders and fattened up.

The fairground day, as it was named, was now an annual event and was popular with the city folk, and Mr O'Flaherty. It was the talk of the city for weeks before and after.

The Christmas trees brought in a tidy sum every December and the dogs were used nightly to ward off thieves. One morning, in early December in the first year, over one hundred trees had been chopped down overnight by thieves. Everyone was furious so it was never allowed to happen again!

Fishing was now hooking a regular number of anglers, and stocks of fish had been purchased from a local hatchery: trout and carp.

Then came trouble...

Chapter 20
Someone Was Not Pulling
Their Weight!

One morning, Thomas Jameson was asked to appear at a hastily convened committee meeting. His wife, Mildred, came with him. Both were looking worried.

Charlie began: 'Tom, we are sorry to have to bring up this subject, but you have been reported to be not pulling your weight, as far as the work here is concerned.'

'Me?! I'll have you know I do my share. Who has snitched on me? Who?' Thomas demanded to know.

'My Tom works as hard as anyone. As hard as any of you lot, harder even,' his wife shouted defiantly. She was beside herself with rage.

'Nevertheless, complaints have been made and must be investigated,' Charlie said. 'If nothing is seen to be done, the situation will escalate. You can understand what could result… chaos!' Charlie had seen this word in a newspaper and Fred had explained its meaning, and pronunciation.

'Okay, what am I supposed not to have done?' Thomas demanded to know. He was red from his hairline to his shirt collar. He had a good idea why he was there but tried to appear innocent.

'One report said you have sloped off for well over an hour when on gate duty, on several occasions, leaving the other person to do the work. I noticed you missing myself last week. Where were you?'

'I, erm, had a call of nature, that's all,' Thomas said.

'He cannot be blamed for that,' Mildred stated forcefully.

'For over an hour, on several occasions?' said Charlie. 'The others are on the verge of refusing to share the rota with you.'

'Well, I was taken bad, wasn't I?' Thomas added hopefully. The committee members were sceptical.

'The point is, Tom, that you will have to improve or, under the agreement you signed when we came here, you will be told to leave. None of us want that but the ball's in your court,' said Charlie. This was a saying he had picked up from TV.

'Humph! I am not happy about this, not happy at all. If I am snitched on again, I'll want to know who said what.'

'That would not be permitted. Just make sure you are not in this position again. If you are "taken bad", let the person on duty know, or phone me and we can arrange cover. Do not just disappear. You may go,' Charlie said.

The Jamesons stormed out of the room.

'Who do they think they are?' said Mildred loudly as they exited slamming the door.

'Throw us out! Not without a lot of trouble they won't,' Thomas declared. 'I'll go to my lawyer.' Word soon spread through the Hall folk. Supper time that evening was so quiet, dropping pins were making an awful racket.

After a few days, tempers cooled, slightly, but there was still an "atmosphere" about the place.

Daisy said to Charlie, 'The Jamesons are still mad, Charlie.'

'Can't be helped, dearest. You heard the complaints. We could not just ignore them,' Charlie replied. 'Give an inch and some people will take a mile, or two!'

Thomas and Mildred never missed an opportunity to get a dig at a committee member. 'Look at Charlie Beaumont, standing there with his two arms the one length. And he dared to say I wasn't pulling my weight,' said Thomas, often.

Ill feeling festered, and some guests made comments to that effect in the visitors' book.

Eventually, Charlie felt something had to be done. He called a meeting of all the adults one evening. The older children cared for the toddlers. There were now several more on the premises, so a room had been converted into a nursery.

'Right. Is everyone here? Good. I think you all know why I called this meeting.' Some looked embarrassed; the Jamesons looked smug.

Charlie continued, 'There has been growing tension in our midst this past few weeks. One of our number was interviewed by the committee regarding skiving off work. You all know how important it is that we all do our bit to keep this place going.' Murmurs and nods of agreement.

'So far, we have managed to pay all our bills and get this place sorted. However, now our guests are commenting adversely on the situation, and worse, as a result, some may not return. This could mean a disaster for our future and cannot be tolerated.' There were murmurs of agreement. The Jamesons were silent. They knew Charlie was right.

113

'So, as from now, this stops. Anyone, and I mean anyone, who continues to disrupt things will be shown the door. And will forfeit their shares. The committee has agreed this. Do I make myself clear?' Charlie looked around at every face. He hated laying down the law but, on this occasion, it was necessary.

There were more nods and murmurs of agreement and two red faces.

All was well after this. Everyone put the incident behind them.

Unfortunately, the peace did not last.

Chapter 21
Disaster Strikes!

One warm sunny morning, two of the Porter kids, Geoffrey and Lionel, decided to go swimming, despite numerous warnings not to go near the lake. Denver, their younger brother, was with them, but sensibly decided it was too dangerous and returned to the house to tell his parents.

'Yah, tell-tale!' Lionel shouted at him. Geoffrey laughed.

The two lads threw off their clothes, put on their swimsuits and jumped in off a jetty, as they thought they could swim well enough. Unfortunately, they did not take account of the weed in the water which had grown profusely in the warm weather. Geoff's foot got caught in the weed and he began to panic and struggle. Lionel bravely tried to help him, but Geoff's flailing arms dragged him under.

'Let go of me, or we'll both drown!' Lionel cried, but Geoff was too panicked to listen and grabbed his brother round the neck, and Lionel was not strong enough to get free.

By the time the parents and a few other adults arrived, both boys appeared drowned. Their seemingly lifeless bodies were hauled out and laid in the grass. The adults tried to resuscitate them while one phoned for an ambulance. Denver was standing nearby crying his eyes out. Sadie tried to comfort him. The other children were kept in the house. Little faces appeared at the windows.

By the time the ambulance arrived, there was little hope, and everyone feared the worst. The paramedics worked quickly for some time but eventually, they were forced to give up. The two little, lifeless bodies were taken away to the Coroner's mortuary.

Of course, the Porters were distraught, as were all the residents. A deep gloom settled over the house.

As there were only a few guests at the time their stay was not disrupted, but Sadie telephoned those who had booked in advance for the next fortnight to cancel, explaining the tragic circumstances. A message was put on the answering machine to the effect that no bookings would be taken for the following two weeks and apologising for any inconvenience.

Next day, Gwen Porter, through her sobs, told her husband Benny she wanted to go home.

'But this is home, Dearest,' he replied. 'We've nowhere else to go.'

'No, I mean back to London. I want to take our other three kids back there. We should never have come here. And I want to bury Lionel and Geoffrey there too, beside my mum and dad.'

She would not be reasoned with, so Benny told the others of their decision. He phoned some friends in London so they could find temporary accommodation.

Once the bodies were released by the Coroner, they arranged for a funeral director to bring the two boys to London.

The committee voted to give them a departing gift of money, as well as the value of their shares, to tide them over until they got settled. Everyone turned out to wave goodbye. The remaining Porter children, Susan, Denver and Charlotte waved goodbye to their friends. A lot of tears were shed by men, women and kids, and several of the folk travelled later to London for the funeral.

For many days, everyone went about their duties with a heavy heart for things still needed tending to. Then came some good news!

Daisy Beaumont announced that she was pregnant, with twins. 'Charlie, do you remember the old saying: "Two heads are better than one"?'

Charlie nodded. 'Yes, that's an old Scottish song: "Twa heids are better than yin".'

She said, 'I am expecting twins!' Charlie's jaw hit the floor.

When he got used to the idea Charlie was like a dog with two tails. All the folk greeted the announcement joyfully and soon, baby clothes and toys began to appear. Charlie still ran the fish stall in the market, but Daisy took on lighter work in the house and vegetable garden for a few months.

And so, a few days before the expected time, two new little Beaumonts were born, one of each, named Dante and Daphne, after the Whittingtons who were close friends. They were also Godparents at the baptisms in the cathedral, as was traditional with the many dukes' children down the years. The Second Duke had donated a large white marble font to mark the occasion of the birth of his eldest. The Dean presided and joked it had been a long time since he had "done two for the price of one". Everyone laughed. The Hall folk also promised to be more regular in attendance at services, which some did. Others did for a while but fell away after a few weeks.

Fred, however, was not pleased: he just grunted every time someone spoke to him for days.

'I think he is a bit jealous, now the babies are getting all the attention,' said Sadie.

'He'll get over it in a day or two,' said Daphne Whittington, and indeed, Fred soon became the protective big brother for his siblings. He was even seen quite often pushing the double pram around.

Chapter 22
Disaster Strikes Again

Things progressed at the Hall. All the renovation work had been completed so, except for maintenance work, the fishery and the garden, most of the folk were free to follow other work where they could get it. They covered most of the county and beyond.

Lee Wu's restaurant in the city was doing well, employing several from the Hall and some locals. He opened it from noon till eleven p.m.

All the stalls did good business in four towns every week, and jobs for plumbers, carpenters, mechanics, glaziers and others were usually in demand. Uel Middleton got a job as a "bouncer" at a nightclub in Frampton-on-Thames, a neighbouring town, which was much larger than the city of Market Barton.

Market Barton had been granted a city charter during the reign of King Charles II, in 1660, for loyalty to the Royalist cause during the English Civil War. The town had supplied fifty cannon, thirty cavalry and a regiment of infantry, musketeers and pikemen, for the king's army.

The committee treasurer, Sadie, reported a really healthy financial balance. The Porters' names had been removed from the mortgage agreement.

All those who did work outside had been warned to keep their taxes declared honestly, as most transactions were cash in hand. 'We do not want to see any of you carted off to the clink in handcuffs,' Sadie had stated.

Then disaster struck again.

Three of the younger children, Samuel, Christopher and James Wu, one autumn evening, had found an old candle in a cupboard and thought it would be fun to see it burning in the dark.

'Let's get this lit tonight. It'll be fun,' said Chris, who was always the leader in mischief.

'Don't tell any of the adults, 'cause they'll take it away,' added Sam.

They managed to get a box of matches from the kitchen and lit the precious candle. Unfortunately, they forgot to use a candlestick, being unused to this form of lighting.

Predictably, the candle fell over and the flame set fire to some bedclothes material. It quickly flared up and the children squealed and tried desperately to extinguish it. Their efforts only spread the flames until soon the bed and curtains were well alight.

An older child, Mary Whittington, in the room next door, heard them crying and shouting and rushed in. She immediately grabbed the three kids and hauled them out of the room and slammed the door. Another child, Arwen Lyttle, set off the fire alarm quickly, as they had been taught in regular fire drills. Fire alarm points were placed at regular intervals in the corridors.

Soon, they were shepherding all the kids down the old servants' stone stairway which led to the kitchen area: the comings and goings of servants in the past had been kept out of sight of the nobility as much as possible.

The adults, meanwhile, had all assembled in the entrance hall and ensured the guests had evacuated their rooms. Charlie and some of the men had raced upstairs to the top floor and were relieved to see the last of the children exiting down the other stairs.

The whole crowd then went out and gathered on the lawn, as it had been designated the assembly point for such an event. Sadie meanwhile had telephoned the fire service.

'Just as well we did fire drill,' said Daisy when everyone was thought to be out.

'Yeah, isn't it just,' Charlie said with a sigh of relief.

'Where's our Dwayne?' cried Mary Middleton frantically. 'DWAYNE!' she yelled.

Uel Middleton joined in the shouting: 'DWAYNE... DARREN.'

'I'm okay, Dad, I'm safe,' said their son, Darren, who ran up. 'Last time I saw Dwayne he was going for a bath.'

'Oh no! Dwayne must be still in there!' Mary shouted frantic with worry.

Panic ensued! Everyone started shouting, 'DWAYNE!' Suddenly, someone saw a very anxious head appear at a window on the upper floor, just to the right of the front entrance. Dwayne had been having a bath with loud heavy-metal music playing on earphones, so he never heard the alarm. He did not find out about the fire until he went to open the bathroom door.

'HELP!' he shouted. 'Mum, Dad, I'm trapped! Help!'

'We must go in to rescue him,' Charlie shouted.

'No, no, it's too dangerous,' cried Daisy.

Charlie replied, 'We've got to do something! Anyone got a blanket? He could jump into it.' Just at that moment, after what felt like hours, the fire tenders arrived, and numerous hoses were soon directed at the flames. The lake came in handy, and hoses snaked down to the water. Unfortunately, the fire had spread from the Wu kids' bedroom into the roof-space, and the dry timbers soon were alight. The fire spread rapidly along the front rooms of the building.

Charlie told the fire chief that one lad was still in there, pointing at the window where Dwayne was.

Some fire fighters tried to make their way up the stairs, but the flames drove them back, and the staircase then collapsed.

'There is no alternative, the lad will have to jump! Our turntable ladder won't reach the window. The truck can't get close enough because of the terrace,' said the chief.

The chief ordered his men to deploy a circular rubber sheet under the window. Meanwhile, others were hosing the building to stop the fire spreading to the sides and rear of the premises. The front section was well alight by this time and was beyond their efforts to save it.

Dwayne's father shouted to him to jump. 'Jump, son, it's your only hope!'

'I can't! It's too high!' Dwayne wailed. By this time, he had climbed out of the window onto a ledge.

'You have got to, Dwayne. There is no other way. Our ladders won't reach. Don't worry, we will catch you,' shouted the fire chief.

After some hesitation, Dwayne, in his Batman bathrobe, slippers and underwear, took a deep breath and yelled, 'GE-RONIMO!' and then he jumped!

Professionally, the fire fighters caught him, and he ran to his parents' arms. They were all full of thanks, but the fire fighters hurried to help with the hoses.

'It is all going to be lost,' cried Carol in despair. 'All our work gone up in smoke.'

'Aye, but maybe they can save some of it,' said Quentin Lyttle. 'Let's not give up hope yet.'

The fire service chief came over. 'We think we are getting it under control. But I'm afraid most of the front top floors have been destroyed. Any idea how it started?' The Hall folk looked at each other but nobody knew. Some of the kids looked sheepish.

'Okay, Sam, Jamie and Chris, what do you know?' asked Charlie as kindly as possible. The Wu boys burst into tears.

Mary Whittington spoke up. 'It was an accident, Mr Beaumont. They were playing with a candle—'

'How many times have you been told not to play with fire?' cried Brenda Wu. The kids just cried even more.

'Okay, everyone, be calm,' said Charlie. 'We can talk about this later. The main thing is everyone is safe. We must be thankful for that.' Everyone agreed and hugged the three lads.

'Alright, I will leave you folk, and check on my men,' said the fire chief, and he hurried off.

Chapter 23
'You'll Not Be Stopping in that for a Day or Three'

Mr and Mrs Grimshaw appeared a few minutes later, as did some other neighbours having heard the fire engines and seen the blaze.

'You'll not be stopping in that for a day or three,' said Harry Grimshaw, matter-of-factly.

'You can all come to ours for tonight at least,' said his wife. They had a large, old farmhouse. 'Be a bit of a squeeze but at least it will be out of the weather. It's looking like rain, and those little kiddies have only their pyjamas.'

'Never rains but it pours,' Sadie muttered. 'Thanks, Mrs G. That's very kind of you.'

'Yes, thank you, Mrs G,' said Daisy. Daisy had collected eggs at the farm most days and had enjoyed many cups of tea and chats… long chats. Her real name was Gladys, but everyone called her Mrs G.

'Thank you very much, Mrs G,' said Charlie. 'Okay,' he shouted to get everyone's attention. 'The women and kids head over to the Grimshaws' farm and get the kids to bed as best you can. It will be like camping indoors, kids. And mind you behave yourselves,' he added. The children brightened up at this "adventure".

'Thank you so much,' everyone said to Harry and his missus.

The men remained behind to see what could be done, if anything, when the fire was out.

'Won't be safe to go in there for a while,' said the fire chief. 'My men will have to check the whole building.'

A short time later, most of the men went to the farm too. Charlie and Dante Whittington remained behind sitting in a car, in case of opportunist thieves when most of the fire fighters left.

Next morning, the folk thanked the Grimshaws for their hospitality. The men had shared one large room and the women another. The boys and girls occupied two rooms on the ground floor, though there had been little sleep.

There had been a good breakfast of boiled, fried or scrambled eggs, and bacon with tea, coffee or milk served in shifts. The children loved it: gathering the eggs, cooking them, and sitting cross-legged on the floor munching bacon butties.

There was great relief all round that they were not facing another funeral! 'Walls can be rebuilt, children not so,' commented Mrs Grimshaw wisely, patting Dwayne on the head. He was wrapped in a heavy blanket.

Everyone agreed. Dwayne felt a bit embarrassed with all the attention.

When they arrived back at the Hall, there was still some smoke rising in places. A few fire fighters had remained behind to dampen down the bits in question.

'Oh, what a mess,' cried someone.

'Aye,' said Charlie. 'What the fire didn't get, the water has soaked.'

'I hope our insurance will cover it,' said Sadie gloomily.

'They had better pay up, or we are snookered good and proper,' said Daisy.

'Up a creek without a paddle,' said George McNeil.

'We will worry about that later,' Charlie added gently.

'Now I suggest some of us head over to "Bartonshire Caravan and Mobile Home Sales" and see if we can hire a few mobile homes. As many as possible. There will at least be heating. Might get a discount for bulk,' Charlie continued. It brought a smile to their faces. 'The rest see what you can salvage from indoors when you get the all-clear.'

When noon came, half a dozen neighbours who had phoned each other, arrived with trays of sandwiches and gallons of milk, coffee and tea. Large catering teapots, cups and plates had been borrowed from the parish hall at St John's Church down the road. The minister and his wife pitched in and helped. Soon, everyone was picnicking on the lawn, surrounded by the pieces of furniture and fittings which could be salvaged. Soaked carpets, which were not fire-damaged, were spread out to dry. Fortunately, the rain had not lasted for long and the sun shone down.

Twenty minutes later, a convoy of six large mobile homes arrived. They were all that were available at short notice. Some families had to double up and the children were really excited. 'Cor, just like being on holiday,' said Fred.

After some manoeuvring, the vehicles were placed in a line along the driveway. Charlie called a meeting of all the Hall folk in front of one mobile.

'Right, friends,' he said, 'you all know the situation.' Nods of agreement and sad faces.

'What we need to do is decide the future. I don't know if the house is repairable, but if so, it will cost a lot more cash than we have got in the bank. If the insurance company pays up, and it is a big if, we might be able to. If not, then we are in big trouble.' Everyone looked at each other not knowing what to say.

Sadie spoke up. 'I phoned the insurance company earlier and they are sending a bloke out later today. We should know then one way or the other. At least our premiums were paid up to date, thankfully.'

Charlie continued, 'Thanks, Mum. We have managed to salvage some stuff, but it will have to be dried out. The hoses have soaked the whole front part of the house but the sides and back of the building are intact. We could move in there eventually if we can get it weatherproofed and some heating arranged. Winter is not far away.

'Meanwhile, we can continue with the markets and other jobs.' Most of their market goods had been stored in an old barn which was undamaged.

'"Bartonshire Caravans" have done us a good hire deal,' Charlie continued. 'They have been very generous, but it will still drain our account, though they said they would give us time to pay.' The others nodded in appreciation. 'We are also hoping British Heritage might cough up some more funds, but I don't hold out a lot of hope. Has anyone any comments?'

'Is the house worth repairing? I mean, we could just sell it and the land,' suggested Olivia Anderson. 'Suppose something like this happened again?'

'Well, we could sell, but let's not go there yet, Olivia. We should not decide while we are still in shock. We should know better in a day or two how the land lies, and we can meet again. Besides, we are all safe, which is the main thing. No point in making big decisions while we are all tired and upset,' Charlie said wisely. Everyone seemed happy with that.

The insurance assessor, Mr Basil Simpson-Weaver, arrived after lunch and he looked over the property. 'Do you know how the fire started?' he asked after introductions were made.

'Kids with matches and a candle I'm afraid,' Charlie said. There was no way to avoid the truth as the fire chief would be reporting it anyway.

'Hmm,' the man said, and he wandered off a few yards and telephoned his office. A few minutes later he returned and said, 'Depending on the fire service confirming that as the cause, we feel we can make a payment under "accidental damage".' Everyone was relieved. 'However, it may not cover all the cost of repairs. In fact, looking at that building, I'm afraid it will only be a fraction of your needs, and no doubt your premiums will rise considerably.'

'It will help. Thank you,' Charlie said, and they shook hands. Mr Simpson-Weaver got into his car and drove off.

Just then, they heard car horns beeping and a large green truck arrived, followed by some cars including the Lord Mayor's black limousine. It had the City's Coat of Arms, a crowned lion, on the doors. Several reporters also came along. The Hall folk gaped open-mouthed. 'What's all this?' someone wondered aloud.

The Lord Mayor, Sir Sundar Singh MBE, complete with purple turban, red mayoral robe, and splendid gold chain of office which dated from the reign of Charles II, got out of the limo and shook hands with Charlie and some others. The reporters crowded round, tape recorders whirring and cameras clicking.

The Lord Mayor began, 'Your Grace, Duchess, ladies and gentlemen, girls and boys, we have brought you a gift...' he gestured towards the truck and some men whisked a large blue tarpaulin off '... of some clothing, food and toys. The good folk of the city heard of your loss and collected these garments *et cetera* for your use.'

The Hall folk were amazed and began to applaud. After he recovered from his amazement, Charlie said, 'Mr Mayor, we cannot thank you and the good people of Market Barton enough. As you can see, most of the kids have only their nightclothes left.' They were all still wrapped in blankets loaned by neighbours.

'It is our pleasure, Charlie,' said the Lord Mayor. 'Your folk have brought great benefit to our city, especially Mr Wu's excellent restaurant, "The Golden Dragon". Everyone chuckled as the Lord Mayor rubbed his stomach. 'His curry is most appreciated.' Lee Wu had recently included Indian cuisine in his much-enlarged premises, which now included two former shops on either side. He employed six chefs and numerous assistants.

'Mr Beaumont, Your Grace, how do your people feel about what has happened last night, and about this generous gift?' asked a reporter from the "Barton Weekly News".

'Just call me Charlie. I think I can speak for us all.' Everyone nodded. 'The folk here are naturally gutted by what the fire has done. You are aware, I'm sure, of the hard work they have put in over these past years. However, the generosity shown by our neighbours last night, and now by the good people of the city,' he indicated the piles of gifts, 'is completely humbling. Please include our thanks in your next edition. Thank you to everybody.

'And may I add? We are not beaten!' he declared loudly. 'This is just a setback. I think the Hall will arise again! In fact, I'm sure of it.' Charlie had never made a longer speech in his life, and he felt drained but elated at the same time. Everyone cheered themselves hoarse.

'Thanks, Charlie,' said the reporters, and they took some photos and hurried off back to their offices.

The folk sorted out the donated clothing, ensuring everyone had enough warm clothing. A shoe shop had donated thirty pairs of shoes and trainers in assorted sizes. The food was also distributed to each mobile home as required by the number of occupants. Every available space was crammed with tins of this and that. The kiddies loved their new toys, including teddy bears, as all their favourites had been lost. No time was lost in naming the new bears.

Chapter 24
'It's Been a Long Day'

The fire chief concluded his examination of the property and agreed that the seat of the fire was in the children's room as described. It was a formality really.

'The fire chief has confirmed the source as being the candle in the Wu boys' bedroom,' Charlie said. This information was passed on to the insurance company.

That evening, all the adults crowded into the Beaumonts' mobile home and discussed what to do next.

Charlie began, 'The other three sides of the building are okay, apart from smoke and some water damage. The fire didn't do too much damage there. So, I want to suggest that we get some builder to put a tarpaulin over the front area to preserve what is left, and partition off the rest of the building. Then we can move into the sides and rear until such times, hopefully, as we can get the front repaired. Obviously, it is going to take months, and with winter coming it is going to be rough.

'The rooms in the rest of the building are still largely unfurnished and undecorated, but at least are dry and reasonably comfortable. Any comments?'

'Have you a builder in mind, Charlie?' asked Uel Middleton.

'No, but we can ring round a few in the morning, but knowing builders, we shall have some coming around looking for the tender.'

'I don't think I want to go through all that decorating again!' said Edith Higginson with a sigh.

'Me neither,' added Brenda Wu. 'Is it really worth all the bother? Could we not just live in the remaining bit all the time?'

'We couldn't just leave the front as it is a listed building, and especially with children around. It would be too dangerous as it is bound to deteriorate,' said George McNeil.

'Wow, that's a big word for you, George,' said Charlie laughing. Everyone laughed.

'Deteriorate? Yeah, suppose it is,' said George. 'All this country air must be good for my brain,' he chuckled.

'Could we demolish the front like they did at Woburn Abbey, I think it was, years ago?' asked Daisy.

'I doubt if British Heritage would agree. That must have been before they introduced building grades and regulations for historic buildings,' said Sadie. 'We would have no main rooms for eating, or the bed and breakfast. We will have to cancel the bed and breakfast for the foreseeable future anyway. Many people who have bookings have already phoned or texted enquiring about what we are doing.

'How is the kitchen for damage by the way?'

'It looks very good,' replied Lee Wu. 'Not damaged at all. Only water on floor. We can use still.'

'We can use the kitchen and the rooms on the ground floor in the remaining building as far as possible for eating, then,' said Carol. 'It will be a squeeze, but we will need heating though.'

'We might just have to get some sort of temporary heating set up. And get some other rooms in some order for the kids. The bathrooms and toilets are fewer, but I'm sure we can manage,' said Charlie.

'The sooner we can return these mobile homes the better,' Sadie said. 'Every penny counts as they say.'

'Okay, all agreed?' said Charlie. Nods all around. 'Okay, let's hit the sack. It's been a long day.' There was much chatter as they all went to their own mobile homes. Soon, all went quiet as everyone went to sleep.

Chapter 25
'Do We Have Enough Cash to Give the Go-Ahead?'

The children were allowed the day off school the next day as it was a Friday anyway. They all helped clear away the debris around the front of the building. Nobody was allowed inside though Fred was eager to "go exploring". Daisy soon put that idea out of his head.

Two contractors arrived on cue as Charlie had predicted.

'Don't forget, all structural stuff will have to be as was in the original. British Heritage will insist on that,' said Charlie.

After touring the ruin to see what's what the contractors, each submitted an estimate after much chin scratching and 'Hm, this is going to be pricey, mate,' and 'We could do that, but it'll cost you,' and similar comments.

Charlie thanked them and said he would be in touch, and the committee met in a mobile home to discuss the offers.

Daphne-Isabelle Whittington had been elected to the committee in place of Gwen Porter and was now secretary.

Sadie, who was still treasurer, said, 'Both estimates were very steep, but we will have to do something. We have no other option.'

'Do we have enough cash to give the go-ahead?' asked Alexander.

'Yes, but it will be tight. Unless we get another grant, it will be tough going,' said Sadie. 'Living on a shoestring as they say.'

'Mr Bert Harbison of Barton Construction, says he would block off the two ends of the building to separate the sides from the front and rig a temporary roof over the whole front,' said Charlie.

'That sounds sensible,' said Harry Dunlop.

'What does the other bloke, Kennedy, say?' asked Carol.

'Pretty much the same. Both say it will be a long job,' said Charlie. 'But builders will always say that.'

'We will need to tie them down to a time limit, or it could drag on for years,' said Sadie.

'Barton Construction offers the lower price by twenty thousand pounds, so all in favour raise your hands,' Charlie said.

It was unanimous.

'Provided he can start straight away,' said Sadie.

'And provided he is willing to trust us to get the money needed,' Daisy added feeling pessimistic.

'Okay, I'll phone him,' said Charlie. 'He knows the situation and has said he is willing to go ahead and will give us a reasonable time to pay. The publicity will be good for business he said.'

'Now,' Charlie continued, 'I want to suggest we offer the grazing land to Mr Grimshaw for sale, at a reasonable price which he can't refuse! He has been hinting at that instead of rent for years. We could just buy milk and stuff from him as we need,' said Charlie. 'With some of the kids, sorry, young people, going away to university we will need less food.'

'Good idea to sell the land. I second that,' said Thomas Jameson.

'All in favour say aye?'

'Aye,' said all.

'The ayes have it! The ayes have it! Carried unanimously,' said Charlie grinning. He and Fred had been watching a House of Commons vote on the news.'

Chapter 26
Things Progress

'Well, we have got a great price for the grazing land. So, if you all agree, I propose we put some of it towards clearing part of the mortgage, if we have enough to pay the builders,' Charlie told the assembled Hall folk.

'Sounds like a good idea,' said Uel Middleton. 'It will be one less burden round our necks.' Everyone agreed heartily.

'Okay, I will see the bank manager tomorrow,' Charlie said. 'It will save on interest payments.

'Also, the builders are making satisfactory progress on the restoration work. It is fortunate the roof was slated and not lead, as many old buildings are. Tons of molten lead would have done a lot more damage as you can imagine.

'As the sides and rear of the building have been screened off from the work area we can safely move into the undamaged rooms. It will be a bit uncomfortable at first, but we can hack it.'

'We can return these mobile homes,' added Sadie. 'That will save a few pounds.'

'We can rough it for a while,' commented Daisy.

Those with carpentry skills made beds and furniture. Others renovated stuff bought cheaply at auctions.

British Heritage contributed some cash once again to the restoration work and so, when the builders were finished two years later, there was enough money to pay them. Once more they began decorating the front part of the building.

'Back to square one... more decorating,' said Annie McNeil.

Sadie put the website back up, telling prospective guests they would be back in business from the next spring. Bookings flooded in as there had been much publicity in the media.

'Our finances are looking up with deposits from guests,' Sadie reported at the next committee meeting.

'Yes, at last, the future is looking much better,' Charlie said.

'Barring accidents!' commented Daisy, gloomily.

In time, all the ground floor rooms were opened for guests. The ones at the sides and rear of the building were a bit cheaper, or shall we say less expensive, and the central courtyard, accessed by French windows, had been tidied and planted with shrubs. Garden seats and tables were placed for the use of guests, and an old fountain, in the shape of a dolphin with water flowing from its mouth, was restored to working order. Many guests enjoyed balmy summer evenings there.

Chapter 27
The *Grim Reaper* Strikes

Some years passed. The older children left school and some "flew the nest" getting jobs in distant towns. Some had been the subject of bullying and left as soon as they could. A few headed for London. Fred Beaumont, now a tall, athletic young man having taken up a fitness regime, went to university to study politics much to the surprise of his parents. Dwayne and Darren Middleton went to different universities too. Darren still had his heart set on becoming a fighter pilot.

Eventually, Mary, Rose and Lily Whittington also went to different universities.

When Fred graduated and started work in a local accountancy firm, he stood for the Market Barton City Council as an independent, which he won by a landslide. He immediately set about tackling what was seen as money wasted by the council. He was very single-minded when he espoused a cause. Before long, the council was saving money and was able to redirect funds to other needy work. Taxpayers welcomed a reduction in Council Tax, the first ever reduction.

'I don't know where he gets his brains from, but it certainly wasn't me,' said Charlie on many occasions.

'Not from me either,' added Daisy. Charlie and Daisy were so proud of him, cheering wildly when he won an election.

'He's got his head screwed on has that lad. He will be Prime Minister someday, just wait and see,' said not a few.

'It's hard to believe the little boy running around the Hall in short trousers is now wanting to be an MP!' said one of the Hall people.

At the next general election, he was elected as Member of Parliament for Bartonshire East.

Sadie Beaumont died suddenly from a heart attack! The Hall folk were once again in mourning. But this was only the beginning of their trials. Carol Dunlop, Lee Wu and George McNeil followed in quick succession over a period of three weeks when a virus struck. All had been getting elderly. Mary Middleton had had a lingering illness, which was finally ended by pneumonia.

'We are going to be in difficulties,' Charlie told the next committee meeting, after a minute's silence to honour the departed friends. 'None of us adults are getting any younger. There are only sixteen of us left, and the young-uns are moving away rapidly. Our Freddie spends most of the time in London of course, and it is unlikely all of those still at school will stay here forever. Most have ambitions which will take them away. There are bound to be fewer to do all the jobs with the fishing and trees and the dozens of other things needing attention. So, the thing is, has anyone got any suggestions?'

'We could take on some local folk to do some of the work if it becomes necessary, or when it becomes necessary,' said Harry Dunlop. 'I'm getting on a bit and my arthritis does play havoc some days.'

'I know the feeling,' said Charlie grinning. 'Right, that is a good suggestion.'

'We need to set something down in writing. A sort of group Will, if there is such a thing, to take care of every eventuality. Time will come when none of us will be around or capable of looking after the place,' said Daisy. They all nodded agreement.

'I'll see Mr Grimes as soon as possible,' Charlie said. Mr Grimes was the only original partner left in the law firm, though it retained the original name. Both the Grimms had died.

'Okay. If there is nothing else, we can adjourn?'

Mr Grimes came to the Hall and suggested that each person over eighteen be granted equal shares in "Barton Hall Enterprises Ltd". They had decided to call the whole business this. When that person died, his or her shares would be distributed to the others. If a person left voluntarily to live elsewhere the shares would be bought, for those remaining, from funds, and he or she would receive the proceeds. Children reaching the age of eighteen would also receive shares if still a resident and working to contribute to the Hall. Some were already working the market stalls of their parents quite successfully.

So, Mr Grimes drew up an agreement to that effect.

Chapter 28
Death Strikes Again

No sooner had he spoken, at a committee meeting some months later, than Charlie Beaumont groaned and clutched his chest. He slid off his chair onto the floor.

Daisy screamed and rushed to his side. She dropped to her knees and held his hand. 'Charlie, Charlie, what's wrong?'

'Let me have a look,' said Daphne who was a nurse. She felt his pulse which was weak. 'I think he has had a heart attack. Quick, call an ambulance!' She propped Charlie up against the wall and bent his knees. Someone placed a cushion behind him. 'Can you get an aspirin, please?' Daisy hurried to a medicine cabinet. 'Ah, good. That will stop any blood clots,' said Daphne.

Harry Dunlop had already phoned for an ambulance which was not long in coming. The patient was rushed into intensive care, but there was little hope.

A group of friends waited with Daisy in the hospital for about an hour. They all stood as a doctor approached.

'Mrs Beaumont, we carried out an ECG, an electrocardiogram, and attempted resuscitation for some time on your husband, but I'm sorry to have to tell you, Mr Beaumont passed away at eight-fifteen,' said the doctor to Daisy and the others who were waiting anxiously. 'There was nothing we could do. We think he may have been having heart problems for some time, as his heart was in poor condition,' the doctor continued.

'He never said anything, Doctor. He mentioned having what he called heartburn a few times, but that is just like Charlie not wanting a fuss,' Daisy said. Daisy then collapsed and Harry Dunlop, fortunately, caught her. They helped her to a seat.

'I must phone Freddie and Maisy again,' said Daisy after a few minutes. Maisy was living and working in Edinburgh. Freddie was in London. Phone calls had been made to them just after Charlie had been taken to hospital.

A note was passed to the Honourable Member for Bartonshire East, who was on his feet at the Despatch Box speaking in the House of Commons. He was a Front-Bench spokesman for the New Democrat Party, then in opposition. There was a sitting to debate a radical Finance Bill and Fred went pale and stopped abruptly. He sat down, his legs turning to jelly. The Speaker of the Commons, Mrs Abigail Swanson, called a halt to proceedings.

'Mr Beaumont are you feeling unwell?' she asked. Freddie recovered a little, stood and said, 'My apologies to the House, Madam Speaker, but I must leave immediately. It seems my father has been taken seriously ill.'

Everyone gasped and wished Charlie well, from all sides of the Chamber. Everyone knew of Fred's father and his work at the mansion. Many had visited the Hall on occasion.

'I'll drive you,' said his friend and fellow MP Jimmy Marshall. Jimmy, a tall, young man with a neatly trimmed beard, was Member of Parliament for Yorkshire North-West. Fred always travelled by train to London.

Fred was soon on his way home, driven by Jimmy, when he got the call saying his father had "passed away".

'Dad's gone, Jimmy,' he said quietly. A tear trickled down his pale cheek.

'Oh no! I'm so sorry, Freddie,' Jimmy Marshall replied. After a few minutes of silence, he said, 'I suppose that makes you the new Duke, mate.'

'I never thought of that. Still, I wish I weren't,' said Fred sincerely. They passed the rest of the journey in silence.

When they arrived at the hospital at about nine p.m., Daisy and the others embraced him in turn. 'I'm so sorry, son,' she said. 'There was nothing they could do for him. He didn't suffer, which is a blessing. He never regained consciousness.'

'How are you, Mum?' Fred asked.

'I'm okay now. I have got over the shock a little. Let's go home, you look exhausted,' Daisy said. 'You'll come too, won't you, Jimmy? It's getting too late for you to start back to London tonight.'

'Thank you, Mrs Beaumont. If it won't be any bother?' Jimmy replied.

'Call me Daisy. You're like one of the family, Jimmy. Freddie has so often spoken of you. You are very welcome.'

'It's been a long day, with one thing and another,' Fred said.

Back at the Hall, everyone was still up and awaiting news. A reporter had got wind of something and was at the foot of the steps.

Jimmy Marshall told him "politely" to clear off. 'Leave your card and someone will speak to you in the morning,' he added.

'Could someone make up a bed in a spare room for Jimmy, please?' Fred asked. 'You'll stay for a few days, won't you, Jimmy?'

'I'll do it,' said Brenda Wu.

'I will give you a hand,' said Mildred Jameson.

'If I won't be intruding, I'll stay for the funeral,' Jimmy said. 'Can I borrow some necessaries?'

'Of course, you won't be intruding,' said Daisy. 'It'll be a comfort for Fred having you around. We can come up with what you need, toothbrush and such, I'm sure.'

'My girlfriend, Alice, will be here tomorrow sometime,' said Fred. 'She's in Holland at present. I phoned her when we were in the car, and she is catching the first flight in the morning. And I'll phone the funeral director in the morning. We'll bury Dad in the Beaumont family mausoleum beside Granny Sadie.' He then yawned wearily.

'Okay, let's all get some sleep,' said Daisy. She sobbed herself to sleep that night. As did many others, truth be told.

The funeral of the late Tenth Duke was a grand affair. The Lord Mayor, now Sir Larry Ponsonby KG, Bishop Cedric Appleby, and many members of the House of Commons and House of Lords attended. The monarch sent a message of sympathy and was represented by the Lord Lieutenant of Bartonshire, Lady Cynthia Smythe-Truesdale.

The Bishop paid a moving tribute as to how Charlie rose from being a fishmonger to be a Duke and fishmonger, that he never acted grandly and never lost the common touch. How he was loved by everyone in the city and district, and then he addressed the new Eleventh Duke. 'If you are anything like your father, Frederick, you will be a credit to his memory.'

Fred stood and said, 'I hope I can be half the man he was.' Then he thanked everyone for coming and invited those who wished to, to go to the nearby hotel "The Beaumont Arms" for refreshments.

The family and close friends then proceeded to the mausoleum, a great granite pile some twenty feet high, erected by the First Duke in the cathedral grounds. The bones of many Beaumonts lay there, except for the Ninth Duke and family, whose bodies had never been recovered from the sea. A brass plaque commemorated him and his family.

The interment over, they all joined their friends in "The Beaumont Arms".

Chapter 29
A Conflict of Interest?

'Mum, I don't know if I can continue as a Duke and as an MP, too,' said Fred to his mother a few days later. 'My whole political career, such as it is, has been about trying to eliminate poverty and inequality. The media is going to latch on to the duke thing at every opportunity. You know what they're like.'

'Vultures, the lot of them. And you have done a wonderful job, Son,' said Daisy. 'Your party wouldn't have made you Shadow Home Secretary if they didn't think so. If the media is so narrow-minded they can't see that, then too bad. After all, this house is owned by us all, not just the Duke. It is only a title; it does not change you as a person. It certainly never changed your father. I tried often enough,' she laughed. 'Do you remember how he used to say, "Call me Charlie" when someone called him "Your Grace".' Daisy said. Fred chuckled.

'You're right, Mum, as always,' Fred said, and he gave her a big hug. 'I'll go back tomorrow and work twice… no, three times as hard. I'll show them I am my father's son! A duke with a conscience.'

'Wonderful!' said Daisy. 'And Jimmy tells me that so long as you have not sat, nor intend to sit in the House of

Lords, you can still sit in the Commons as an MP. Never forget, Son, the people of Bartonshire East elected you for who you are, and what you have achieved. Tell that to the media!'

Fred and Jimmy returned to London the next day. Alice, a tall, confident young woman, went with them as she also worked in London for a finance firm. She was not quite sure if she wanted to be a duchess, but as Fred had not yet "popped the question" she put it out of her mind or tried to.

When they arrived at her flat, they dropped her off and arranged for the two of them to meet for dinner that evening in the "Ristorante Bellissima" an Italian establishment in Belgravia. They waved goodbye as Jimmy and Fred drove off in Jimmy's little Clio.

Fred and Alice dined at the restaurant that evening. After the main course, while waiting for the dessert course, Fred swallowed a mouthful of wine, stood as he dabbed his mouth with a napkin, suddenly went down on one knee and said, 'Alice, Dearest, will you make life complete… and get wed?'

'Wed? To whom?' she joked with a mischievous smile at the corners of her mouth. She winked at folk at the next table who had all turned around. Fred had been recognised by most patrons.

'To me, of course!' said Fred worriedly, not sure if she was joking, and he produced a large diamond ring. 'I was going to do this earlier but with Dad dying…'

'I understand, Darling. Just let me think a second.' She looked at the ceiling rubbing her chin as if trying to decide.

Fred started to get worried. All the customers and staff, looking on, held their breath.

'Hmm, yes, okay, of course, I will. A thousand times yes,' Alice said laughing and throwing her arms around his neck.

The restaurant erupted with applause, and the manager and the waiters entered with glasses of champagne for everyone.

'Phew, I am glad you said "yes", or all this champagne would have been wasted,' Fred declared.

Alice laughed and said, 'I am now the happiest woman alive. I love you Frederick Charles George Beaumont.'

'Me too… I mean, I love you too, Alice Mary Beaumont-to-be,' replied Fred. They embraced for several minutes until the manager cleared his throat. Most of the other diners had departed.

'Ahem! Sorry to interrupt, but we will be closing soon.' They all laughed, as Fred looked at his watch, and the pair grabbed their coats and hurried out, after Fred had paid the bill of course.

Chapter 30
Wedding Bells Chimed

The newspaper headlines, two days later, read:

FREDERICK DUKE OF BARTONSHIRE AND MEM-BER OF PARLIAMENT, TO MARRY! Popular MP Fred Beaumont is to wed his long-term girlfriend Alice Mary Camberwell, a real Camberwell Beauty… A close friend of the Duke said the pair will tie the knot in September.

Four months later, in August, the great and the good assembled once more in Market Barton Cathedral, for "the wedding of the century" according to the national papers. Only royal weddings got more coverage. Indeed, one Royal Prince had postponed his planned nuptials so as not to clash, for he knew how popular Fred was.

Fred's younger siblings, Dante and Daphne, the twins, now in their teens, were groomsman and bridesmaid along with Alice's younger sister by five minutes, Isabel, who was identical to her twin. Indeed, Fred had occasionally to hesitate a few seconds to be sure he was speaking to the right sister. Alice had a freckle on her nose!

Jimmy Marshall was the Best Man of course. 'No show without Punch,' he quipped.

An extensive display of photographs appeared in every top glossy magazine. 'Now you really are famous, Fred,' joked Jimmy. 'In the glossies!'

The couple honeymooned in Hawaii and then moved into an apartment in London, which was convenient for their work. They stayed in the Hall for weekends as often as possible to stay connected with the folk there. And, of course, because Fred's constituency work made it necessary for him to be on hand at least one day a week. There was always a queue for his "surgeries".

'GOVERNMENT IN CRISIS!' yelled the headlines one eventful Tuesday morning. Due to three unsuccessful by-elections leaving no majority in the Commons, and a disastrous financial scandal, the Prime Minister, the Right Honourable Donald Turnbull, of the Progressive Party was forced to call a General Election.

Fred's New Democrat Party went all out to win. Fred's face was on television several times a day.

When interviewed, the inevitable question of the Dukedom as a conflict of interest was thrown at Fred, to which he replied: 'My father was a fishmonger, and I am the son of a fishmonger. He never browbeat people with his title and neither do I. Next question!'

The New Democrat Party waited in anticipation as the results came in early on the Friday morning after the election. By six a.m., they had a clear majority, and the newly elected Prime Minister prepared to visit Buckingham Palace to be received by the King.

The Right Honourable Frederick Charles George Beaumont MP emerged from the meeting and waved to the crowd. The New Democrat Party former leader, John Black, had stepped aside in favour of a younger man. 'The job of Prime Minister doesn't need an old codger like me,' he declared. 'MPs should all retire at seventy, I think.' He was seventy-one. Fred was twenty-eight.

'It is a great honour to be in the position to serve the whole United Kingdom. We can all look forward to a bright, prosperous future for everyone, where poverty and homelessness are no more. May God bless us in all our endeavours,' Fred declared in Downing Street outside number ten. A hundred cameras recorded the scene. The news flashed around the world.

Now that he and his wife were living in the official Prime Minister's residence, Fred and Alice were able to contribute to the upkeep of Barton Hall. They stayed there as often as possible to keep their resident status. Their security men really enjoyed the meals laid on in the Hall.

Meanwhile, Edith and Alexander Higginson, and Thomas Jameson had died. The Whittingtons decided to sell their shares and move to the coast for their retirement years, as their three children had all left home. New members were elected to the committee.

The remaining residents now felt it impossible to meet the demands of staffing the whole set-up, so they employed some locals to look after the guests and lure the anglers, who still turned up every season. They were like a club now as everyone knew everyone else. There was even a little seasonal shop selling bait, flies of assorted sizes, and angling paraphernalia set up by an enterprising local. Her little shop grew and grew every season. Tea or coffee was offered free with every sale in chilly weather.

The tree plantation was sold to the Bartonshire Forestry Preservation Society, which found the annual boost to their funds of great benefit. This enabled them to plant areas of indigenous tree species. It also reduced the number of people the mansion folk needed to employ. Plus, they no longer had dogs to guard the property.

Chapter 31
Defeat

Fred's Party won another four terms in government before being ousted by another lot.

'Such is politics,' Fred told the media and his friends, 'the voters do sometimes make mistakes.' He smiled graciously. 'Like many a cricketer, I have had a good innings! Time to pull up the stumps and regroup.'

During his term of office – the longest continuous Prime Minister's term in British history, exceeding even Sir Robert Walpole's twenty years – Fred halved Value Added Tax on British made goods and electric and hybrid vehicles; abolished VAT on home-heating fuels*, VAT on electronic books (which had been imposed by the previous Party), and on food sold in restaurants and cafés; greatly reduced fraudulent claims for benefits, including fraud amongst Members of Parliament; reduced the percentage of unemployment to single figures throughout the United Kingdom. No longer were whole families living on the dole for generations. *Fossil fuels were rarely used for domestic heating now because of climate change regulations.

Homelessness was also tackled rigorously. City Councils had to provide basic shelter for the homeless, and to make every effort to secure them employment as council workers.

New rights for workers were introduced, and the "living wage" was increased annually to allow for inflation. All workers with at least one year's service in a factory, or other firm, received a bonus if the firm made a substantial profit, and not just the directors and shareholders. Productivity shot through the roof.

A new hospital was built nearly every year or existing ones extended, to accommodate the growing elderly population.

A new prison was built most years as automatic prison sentences were imposed for carrying guns, knives, or other dangerous substances without adequate justification. Few excuses were deemed as adequate. Consequently, police numbers were doubled in his first five years in office and increased when required thereafter. The military and security budgets were also increased, as was the budget for the pay of medical staff and teachers.

Steps were taken to ensure all medical facilities had adequate supplies in case of an emergency. Few had forgotten the pandemic of 2020 and years following.

As far as was feasible, every child had to have a good standard of reading and mathematics before leaving school. Extra lessons for those falling short were arranged. Vocational and university places for subjects which would benefit the nation were increased. University tuition fees were reduced and finally abolished early in his period of office, as most were never recovered.

He attempted to return the nation to appreciating moral values. No longer were vociferous minority groups, nor individuals permitted to be 'more equal than others,' as George Orwell might have put it, by having their agenda forced on the nation by a compliant judiciary or MPs, thus denying the right of anyone to disagree with them, much less to oppose them. However, any form of discrimination was not acceptable.

Persons were employed on merit and ability alone, not on their background, ethnicity, or other criteria. Things had got to such an extreme that groups were seeking a quota for themselves in every walk of life, from MPs and employment to awards and sports teams. Sports coaches were faced with the impossible task of "pleasing" all sides to the detriment of the team. The previous Olympic team was chaotic.

Judges could ban protesters from public streets if they caused disruption to the general public and imposed stiff sentences. Initially, this caused the police a lot of problems, but vociferous groups soon got the message.

Any moves towards legalising euthanasia and dangerous drugs were thoroughly opposed. The previous government had kowtowed to pressure to move in that direction.

Abortion laws were amended, and strict rules applied. Abortion was no longer a foregone conclusion as it had become literally abortion on demand. The opposition vehemently opposed this, of course. Huge advances in medical care had also made most "abnormality births" a thing of the past, saving many babies.

Most electric power was now produced by wind, solar and wave power. Hydropower generators were operating on most rivers and on shorelines. A few older power stations were retained for emergency use, when wind and sun were unavailable, or when half the nation switched on their kettles at half time in soccer matches.

The House of Lords was made an elected assembly, except for persons who were considered to have "contributed some outstanding service to the country" which was decided by a panel of worthies from various fields. Proportional Representation was introduced for both Houses of Parliament. Voting became compulsory either in person or by post, from the age of seventeen, unless there were medical or other reasons to make this impossible. Complacency had become normal to many voters.

Unfortunately, even Fred's enthusiasm could not reverse some of previous parliaments' Acts of the late twentieth and early twenty-first centuries.

In the year 2051, the Romanov Czars had been reinstated in Russia, when the old, discredited regime was overthrown. Czar Nicholas III, a descendent of the last Czar's relatives, took the throne and instituted sweeping democratic reforms. Russia subsequently joined the European Union in 2062 which had been enlarged by this time. The "Eurasian Union" now stretched from the Atlantic to the Pacific Ocean.

Fred's Government led the United Kingdom to join what was now basically a trade federation, with the biggest market for products in the world. British industry thrived after this enabling more reforms.

By the time Fred had lost an election and had then resigned from active politics ten years later, the Hall was down to just a few of the original folk. Fred and Alice, plus three young Beaumonts, all girls, named Amelia, Mollie and Jane, felt it was time to move back permanently and keep the old place ticking over. He decided to concentrate on the bed and breakfast side of the business. Alice was an excellent cook, and with the aid of some staff and a modernised kitchen, the Hall was always full of paying guests. Fred greeted each guest personally as often as possible. They appreciated his personal interest.

Fred then decided to open for wedding receptions and other special occasions. There were hardly enough days in the week to fit everything in, and the Hall was booked up for months in advance.

Many new part-time and full-time staff were employed wearing period costumes. Indeed "Barton Hall Enterprises Ltd" soon became a major employer in the county. Many guests commented that the attention to detail and care by the staff made them feel like Lords and Ladies in times gone by.

The website now ran the slogan, "Experience the luxury of a Georgian Stately Home for yourself."

Chapter 32
End of the Century

Some years passed, and all the original adults from London had died, and most of their offspring had moved away to work, or just to get a change of scenery. Many had felt trapped in the Hall and did not share their parents' love for it.

Johnny Higginson and his wife Doris, his sister Kate and her husband Sebastian Burns, and James Wu with wife Maria, remained as residents, along with their growing families. James ran his late father's restaurant in the city. Sebastian claimed to be descended from the famous Scottish poet Robert Burns, but no one really believed him!

In accord with the communal Will, drawn up many years ago, the shares of the deceased and those who left the house were shared by those remaining. Those living and who moved away were paid from funds for their shares, which gave them a financial start elsewhere. Thus, eventually, Fred and Alice and the other three remaining families became sole owners of Barton Hall.

With all the aspects of the estate: guests, catering, stabling, angling and the annual funfair, the enterprise thrived. The turkey rearing was abandoned as the nation had mostly replaced turkey with lamb or beef at Christmas.

The Beaumonts became wealthy, but their three daughters, Amelia, Mollie and Jane, eventually married and moved away. The other families prospered equally.

Fred had stood for election to a seat in the House of Lords. Being a former Prime Minister, he was offered a seat immediately, but he preferred to be elected. He had declined the offer of a complimentary seat due for his long service as Prime Minister and outstanding contribution to the nation.

Inevitably, Fred died in 2095 in his sleep aged eighty-five. He had hoped to see in the twenty-second century, but it was not to be. Alice survived him by another six years and was still active in running the "family business" up to the end.

Within the late Fred's lifetime, the fortunes of the Dukedom of Bartonshire were restored. Gambling, of course, was strictly forbidden! He would never have countenanced the prospect of history repeating itself in the family. He was also created First Earl of Bartonshire by the King in recognition of his service to the county.

Fred, the only surviving Beaumont, his siblings, Dante and Daphne, having predeceased him, had no sons to inherit the title, so his eldest daughter Mrs Amelia Foxwood's eldest son, George Charles Frederick Rupert Beaumont-Foxwood (who introduced this history), became the new Twelfth Duke and Second Earl of Bartonshire. Amelia and her husband Leonard Foxwood had three sons, George, Victor and Quentin, plus two daughters, Margaret-Ann and Julia. Leonard had unfortunately been killed in a car crash the previous year.

George Foxwood, a sensible lad of eighteen, who resembled his grandfather, Fred, in looks and build, was determined to continue the family enterprise. He had no interest in politics.

After assessing the financial state of the business, he had a good head for financial matters like the late Sadie Beaumont, he began a systematic refurbishment of the rooms. Old paintings were cleaned and restored, and new wallpaper replaced the now ageing stuff put up after the fire. What he referred to as "old tat" shoddy items, were removed. A new statue was erected on the pedestal in the driveway, Daisy, his late great-grandmother, having had the original removed long ago. She would have approved of the new one of Charlie Beaumont in a fishmonger's apron.

Everything was modernised without intruding too much on the history of the building, and the numerous guests commented favourably when they left.

The dining area was enlarged and new plates and other tableware with the Coat of Arms were provided by a local pottery, founded by Olivia Anderson a few years before she died. The Beaumont Pottery now rivalled well-established firms. The local clay was found to be excellent for the purpose.

After the period of refurbishment, George opened the Hall as a full-time hotel. It became a popular tourist attraction, and a free guided tour of the cathedral and places of interest in the city and district was included for those who wished to participate. A minibus was available to transport them.

'Barton Hall Enterprises Ltd' soon expanded as George purchased large houses in other counties to convert into hotels. Many of the nobility could no longer afford the upkeep of large properties and they were deteriorating. Starting in Oxford, then Cambridge, Liverpool, Derby, Edinburgh and many more, George invested wisely. He even opened a hotel in London's West End. 'Back near where it all began,' he joked. It was soon competing with long-established hotels.

A statue of George's grandfather, Lord Frederick Beaumont, Eleventh Duke and First Earl of Bartonshire CBE MP, was erected in the city's Main Street in the year 2100, and was unveiled by Richard, the twenty-year-old Prince of Wales, later crowned King Richard IV.

A stained-glass window, which included the Coat of Arms and family motto, was installed in the Cathedral's south transept to honour Fred's life and contribution to the city and the nation.

The city of Market Barton had expanded rapidly in the past fifty years, swallowing up several local villages in the process. Wise councillors had preserved the old village centres as they had been for centuries. They were pedestrianized. The city was now one of the main centres for tourism and commerce in the country.

Future descendants of the Beaumont-Foxwoods became one of the leading families in the United Kingdom, in the arts, politics, business and other fields, all thanks to the hard work and determination of a little man, and his "missus", from Gasworks Street, London.

Well, reader, that brings the family saga up to the twenty-second century. I hope you enjoyed reading it.

I have added a brief summary of a rather unusual event in our history. It follows this one, so do read on. *Au revoir* for now, I need a cup of tea!

George Beaumont-Foxwood. (Duke of Bartonshire).

Ashes to Ashes

Chapter One
The Body!

The headline in the "Daily News" one Tuesday morning in June of the year 2084 read:

CORPSE CONCEALED IN CATHEDRAL. The remains of a person, believed to be male, were discovered yesterday during renovation work being conducted in Market Barton Cathedral, in the county of Bartonshire. A local archaeologist, who was working at the cathedral, has estimated the death occurred approximately forty to fifty years ago.

The Dean of the cathedral informed our reporter that extensive building work was carried out in that area, the north end of the transept, in 2040, due to dry rot being discovered.

Many people still read the traditional printed newspaper, although modern electronic methods had been in use for many years, including hologram "celebrities" reading any parts the viewer wished. You could have Napoleon Bonaparte, Oliver Cromwell or Charles Dickens reading the news, or the weather forecast, in any language! Often with amusing results.

Near the city centre, St Oswald and St Theobald's Cathedral, the fourth largest in England, stood on a low hill overlooking the upper reaches of the River Thames, which ran through the southern part of the County of Bartonshire. It was a large twelfth-century edifice with three slender spires.

Detective Inspector Irvine Gills, of the Bartonshire Constabulary, was leading the investigation of the "Corpse Concealed in the Cathedral" as the press had dubbed it. Reporters had assumed the person had been murdered.

Detective Inspector Gills was a short, about five feet two inches, well-upholstered man (some might say fat) of forty-five years of age, with rapidly thinning hair and a pear-shaped head due to his fat jowls. He habitually wore a grubby tweed suit and red bow tie, usually askew. He had investigated many deaths in his time, but this was the first ecclesiastical one. He was accompanied by Detective Sergeant Sidney McCormick who did most of the "leg work" which Gills hated.

'Well, Mr Thompson,' Gills showed his warrant card and addressed the local archaeologist who had been called in by the Cathedral Chapter, as he had been working nearby on recently uncovered stonework and ancient burials in the Cathedral Close, 'What can you tell me about the...erm...deceased?'

'You are right, Inspector *Jills,* he is indeed deceased,' Thompson chuckled. Gills was not amused. 'Well, anyway,' Thompson continued, 'he was male, judging by the pelvis and femur bones, aged between twenty-five and thirty I would think, five feet ten inches tall at an estimate, brown hair,' there was some still *in situ*, 'well built as his bones look quite heavy. He is certainly not ancient as he was wrapped in plastic sheeting, as you can see.' He chuckled. 'Most of my skeletons have been dead for a few hundred years at least, like King Richard III, wasn't it, who was found under a car park some years ago.' Gills ignored the history lesson.

'Hmm, a comparatively recent burial then, and it's Gills, as in fish. Our pathologist will examine the remains in due course. Thank you for your assistance, Mr Thompson. You may go now, but leave your phone number with my Detective Sergeant, if you would,' said the inspector. He nodded towards McCormick who was writing busily. 'And not a word of the condition of the deceased to anyone, especially the press.' *It would have been better if he had not been near the remains contaminating them, but too late now,* Gills thought.

'Certainly, Inspector. My lips are sealed like King Tutankhamun's tomb.' Gills had never heard of King Tut, so he just grunted.

Thompson took his leave, and an hour later, the scene-of-crime officers from Scientific Services began to photograph the skeleton, its "shroud" of plastic sheet, and any bits of evidence before removal.

Gills spoke to their chief, Jack Stuart, a man covered in white forensic overalls and boots to prevent contamination. 'What do you make of it, Jack? It is obviously a suspicious death. Bodies don't normally get buried in churches these days. Certainly not wrapped in plastic.'

'Well, Irvine, good to meet you again by the way.' Gills nodded in agreement. 'Foul play without a doubt, though you don't need me to tell you that. Poor bloke didn't bury himself! Looks like the skull at the back has been caved in by a blow from something heavy. So, he was hit from behind obviously. I did not want to disturb the remains too much as yet. I will be able to tell you more back in the mortuary when I have a better look.'

'Hmm, I'll let you guys get on with it. Call me when you have any more info, Jack.' Gills made a "phone me" gesture with his thumb and little finger.

'Sure, Irvine, no problem. Shouldn't take long. See you later.' Stuart began to whistle softly as he worked. An unfortunate habit in the circumstances. His colleagues were used to his ways.

Gills turned and walked over to the Cathedral's Dean, The Very Reverend Francis Morris, who was waiting in a pew down the nave, looking extremely upset. The Dean stood.

'Dean Francis, I presume, if that is your correct title. I'm Detective Inspector Gills. Could you shed any light on the history of repairs to this part of the building, please?' he said as they shook hands.

The Dean was a tall, thin man with a dignified air, wearing a "dog collar" and cassock. Many members of the clergy had abandoned the traditional garb even in the Church of England. Casual wear was the choice of many with only a name badge to denote their status. Dean Francis abhorred such informality. 'Unbecoming to the office of clergy,' he called it.

'Yes, Dean Francis, or just Dean is fine, Inspector. Obviously, this occurred many years before I was appointed Dean here, but I have made a few enquiries. Repair work was needed in this area back in early 2040 due to dry rot in the floorboards, I've been told. It seems it was a lot worse than first thought once they started work. That is usually the way with these things.

'The cathedral was floored with wood sometime in the dim and distant past. Maybe to save money. I suspect some local lord owned a sawmill, saw the chance to line his pocket, and sold the wood. Most cathedrals have stone floors.' Gills nodded as Sidney McCormick took notes. Gills was glad of this because his handwriting was lacking legibility. The Dean continued, 'Anyway, the floor had been replaced, and the seating restored. So, one would assume the unfortunate man, or woman, was interred during this period of work.'

'Hmm, so it would seem,' Gills said. 'Any unexplained disappearances among the cathedral staff at the time, by any chance?' he asked hopefully.

'No, I'm afraid not, Inspector. That would have made your job a lot easier, had that been the case,' the Dean said with a wry grin.

'Yes, but worth a try.' Gills smiled. 'Why was the floor dug up this time, by the way?'

'Oh, I am sorry to say the old problem had reoccurred. We are currently surveying the rest of the building as you can see. We will need to lay stone or concrete this time the builder suggested.' He indicated various places on the floor in the huge nave lined with large stone pillars. The walls were covered in monuments to the great, mostly wealthy, people of the city. 'It could land us with a lot of extremely expensive repairs,' the Dean replied gloomily. 'Stone costs the earth. Excuse the pun.' Gills just let it pass.

'Who, if anybody, would have been working here forty or so years ago?' asked Gills.

'Oh, they would have to be in their sixties at least now. So, most would be retired, or dead, I should think,' the Dean replied. 'Unless you included the choristers. Some of them are getting on a bit. I would like to ask a few of them to sing an

"Amen" to their last anthem, but I haven't the courage, I'm afraid.' He shrugged his shoulders and smiled sheepishly.

'Hmm, that does not really help much,' Gills added. 'Can you round up all the staff for a general meeting, please? And any choristers who are, as you say, getting on a bit,' Gills grinned. 'Omit choristers who are under forty-five. And get me a list of any retirees who are still alive if you can, please.'

'Yes, certainly, Inspector, I'll get on the phone to as many as possible,' the Dean replied. 'Most will have heard through the grapevine anyway by now. This city is like a village in that respect.'

'Thank you, Dean. We will probably need to speak to you again.'

'I will be around somewhere, I'm sure. There is always something cropping up needing my attention. Thankfully, few dead bodies,' the Dean said with a smile.

Chapter Two
Interviews

Later that day, all the current older cathedral staff and older choir members had been assembled.

'How many of you were employed or serving here back in around 2040?' Gills asked.

Six hands went up.

'Okay, will the rest give your names and contact details to my officer, then you may go. We will contact you later if necessary. You six folk, please follow me into the vestry,' Gills said. The half dozen obediently followed him with worried expressions on their faces.

When all were seated, Gills asked each in turn who they were, what was their job in 2040, and if they had any inkling of a missing person.

'I am Joshua Robertson, the sexton,' said the first man, a little stooped man of at least seventy years, if not more. His head and chin were covered in a fuzz of grey hair and his remaining three teeth looked like tombstones. 'I've been a bell-ringer and gravedigger for this here cathedral since I were a lad, I have. I didn't dig that bloke's grave though,' he added hurriedly. 'And I have an apprentice lad what does the digging now. But he be too young to have done a murder.'

'Don't worry, Mr Robertson,' said Gills. 'I am only getting some background facts. What age were you forty years go?'

'Forty years younger than I be now, Inspector,' Robertson chuckled. Gills frowned. *Everyone's a comedian around here,* Gills thought. The other five smiled despite the occasion. Robertson resumed, 'I was only seventeen when I started and a right skinny little lad I was too. I had to avoid drains or I would have fallen in,' he joked. The others tittered. 'I was thirty-three in 2040.

'Mr Slowe, old Albert Slowe, was the sexton then, and mighty slow he was too. Took him ages to dig a grave it did, but he did a good job. Very neat worker, very neat indeed. Wasn't he neat?' he looked around at the others. They all nodded dutifully in agreement. 'Yes, very neat. No mess left after we filled in t' grave, I can tell you. You would never have known we were a-digging at all.'

Gills was losing the will to live. *This will take weeks if they are all like him.* He thought. 'Can we keep to the point please, Mr Robertson? Can you recall any unusual happenings, anybody not turning up for work, or just anything unusual at all at the time the transept was being repaired? No matter how trivial.'

Robertson thought for a moment. 'Nope, sorry, Inspector. Nothing comes to mind. I remember well the work going on. There was a big plastic sheet what hung over the transept to keep the dust from flying about, like what there is now. Still were some dust what escaped though. Quite a lot in fact. I remember having to dust half the building afore Sunday matins. Made me sneeze something awful, it did. That's because there was a slit in the middle of the sheet so folk could come and go without having to go outside.'

'So, a person could have moved from the cathedral nave into the transept?' Gills asked.

'Oh, yes, they could. D'you think that's what the murderer did, Inspector?' asked Robertson eagerly.

'I'll ask the questions if you don't mind,' Gills said rather sharply. 'I am only trying to build a picture for the time being. Thank you, Mr Robertson. Who's next?' Gills was feeling grumpy having to endure Robertson's wittering. Sid McCormick was hoping his boss would remain calm.

'I am Ruby Jones, Mrs Jones,' a woman in her sixties spoke up. She was tall and thin, her hair in curlers and wrapped in a striped headscarf. 'I have been a cleaner here for over forty-five years, sir.'

'And do you remember the renovations some forty years ago?' asked Gills.

'Do I remember them rennyvations? Oh yes, I certainly do. I had only started here shortly before. Working for about two months they were. Never done dusting I was, as Josh has said. An' no extra pay neither!' She got nods of agreement from the others. 'Not that we do it for the pay, of course! "Better a doorkeeper in the House o' the Lord, than dwell in the tents o' the wicked," as the Bible says,' she added. Nods of agreement from the others.

'And do you recall seeing anything unusual, Mrs Jones?' Gills asked, trying to keep things moving on the subject.

'Not that I can remember, sir. They just came and went each day, except Sundays, of course. They worked Saturdays in order to finish as soon as possible, in time for Easter, like. The Bishop was to hold a special anniversary service that

Easter, as I recall. For the founding of the Cathedral, way back in King what's-his-name's time. Me and my colleagues arrived each morning early to do a bit of cleaning, afore the morning service. The workmen took a break while matins was on. I think evensong was delayed and held after they finished each evening, if I remember correctly,' said Mrs Jones. Nods from the others.

'They held services every day?' asked Gills.

'Aye, that they did, sir. These choir men must have been worn out,' she added. More nods of agreement from the choristers.

'Are any of your colleagues from that time still here?' Gills looked around the folk assembled.

'Lizzie here was with me,' Mrs Jones tapped the lady beside her on the shoulder.

'Can you tell me who you are?' Gills asked the woman, as he was not getting much information from Mrs Jones.

'I'm Elizabeth Baker, Inspector zur. Lizzie to me friends. We two are the only ones still alive from those days, zur.' She was short and stout, the opposite of her friend.

'Can you add anything to what Mrs Jones has told me?' the inspector asked, trying to avoid another long speech.

'I am sorry, but that be 'bout it, zur. It being a long time ago, and nothing unusual comes to mind,' Mrs Baker said. 'If anything occurs to me, I'll be sure to let you know, zur.'

'Thank you, Mrs Baker. Who's next?' asked Gills.

'Willie Ferguson, from t'choir, tenor,' said the first man.

'Me too. Andy Todd's the name, bass,' the second man said.

'Albert Bernard Toal, Bert to my friends,' said the third.

I see what the Dean meant by getting on a bit, Gills thought. All three were in their seventies or eighties.

'Are you a chorister, too, Mr Toal?' Gills asked.

'That I be, sir. Sixty-five years man and boy. Bass, though I were a boy soprano in me youth.'

'And mighty good he was, too, till his voice broke. Not so good since,' Ferguson chuckled. 'Won all sorts of medals for his singing, he did. I remember him in the front row.'

'Yep. Got medals for me singing I did, back in them days. Went to Wales a few times to the National Eisteddfod. Won every time I did,' Toal added.

'Right, to save keeping you all much longer, can any of you three recall anything unusual happening, when the repairs were being carried out? Anything at all.' Gills was desperate to avoid a lot of reminiscing from these three.

The men thought for a few moments, then Mr Todd spoke, 'It is probably nothing, but I remember a young lad who used to come in and sit near the front of the building, during choir practices. About twenty-five he was, dark hair, and strong looking, like he "worked out" as they call it. I spoke to him a couple of times when we had a break for a cuppa. Said he liked listening to the singing, but he seemed… he seemed distant, like he was reluctant to say much about himself. I didn't want to pry too much. Anyway, after a few weeks or so, he never came back. Never thought no more 'bout him till now.'

'Aye, I remember him too, now you mention him,' said Mr Ferguson. 'I recall he said he lived out at the Hall, Barton Hall that is, where the Duke still lives. Lots of folk lived there in those days, they did. It's a hotel now, but the Duke's family and some others are still there.'

'Thank you, ladies and gentlemen, you have been most helpful. That could be a lead. I'll be sure to follow it up. Okay, you can all go for now. And no talking to the press, or anyone, about the skeleton or any other information.'

'A skellington? Bones like? I thought it was a body. T'papers said a body was found,' said Mrs Jones.

'No, just bones,' said Gills. 'Leave your contact details, email address or mobile phone number, if possible, with the Detective Sergeant. Just in case we need to follow up something.'

The six filed out, chatting animatedly. Gills was sure everything would be told and retold to everyone they met. He shook his head slowly and chuckled quietly.

Chapter Three
The Hall

Inspector Gills then went back into the transept behind the plastic partition and studied the scene. The remains had been removed, and he stood and pondered the possibilities that had led to this crime.

I have got to see if I can trace that lad from the Hall. If he suddenly "disappeared" it could be an indicator. Could be a red herring, of course, taking me on a wild goose chase, up a blind alley. Why would someone, or anyone for that matter, kill a lad and bury him here? It would be easier just to bury him in the woods or dump the body somewhere. Okay, I'll pay a visit to this hotel, but first I'll go to the mortuary, he decided.

An hour later, saw him talking with Jack Stuart, the police pathologist.

'Morning, everyone. Right, Jack, what have you got for me?' Gills asked.

'Hmm, well, he was male, aged about twenty-eight or thirty according to his teeth, perfect by the way, so there may not be dental records; five feet ten inches tall, dark brown hair, there was some still left, muscular build I would say. Hit on the head once with a heavy object, like a rounded base of something about five centimetres thick like…'

'Like the base of a candlestick?' Gills finished the sentence.

'Exactly. Very handy implement being in a cathedral. Plenty of them about,' said Stuart.

'Yep, but after forty years or so there would be no traces on it… certainly no fingerprints,' Gills mused.

'That would be right. I'll get them examined if you wish,' Stuart said.

'No, don't bother. The killer would have cleaned off any blood and prints. Anyway, they will have been polished a hundred times since, and they will still be there if we need to in the future. It would only prove one was the weapon and would not help trace the killer,' said Gills. 'On second thoughts, get one and match it to the wound just to be certain.'

'Will do.'

'Well,' Gills said, 'that description of the victim ties in with a description of a lad who frequented the cathedral about that time. Clothes, what about his clothes?'

'Something there possibly. Pretty expensive, what's left of them. Dry soil must have preserved them: shirt looks like it was top of the range; trainers, hardly worn so new but again top of the range, socks, jeans, again an expensive brand, and underwear, CKs. That's it I'm afraid.'

'CKs?'

'Yeah, Calvin Klein. They have been trading for years and nearly every guy on the planet has worn them, I'm sure. These ones were expensive, so I would say he was a guy who liked being well dressed. Plenty of money anyway for a guy his age. That's about it, so far,' Stuart said.

'Hmm, well it's a start. Thanks, Jack. I owe you a drink for that… sometime,' Gills grinned.

'A body could die of thirst waiting for you to buy a round,' Jack laughed.

Gills laughed, 'When I win the lottery, perhaps. Which is unlikely because I don't do it,' and they shook hands.

A few minutes' drive into the country took Gills to Barton Hall Hotel. A large sign marked the entrance giving information about prices and fishery opening times.

Gills preferred speaking to someone in person. He could have used the modern emotion-sensitive video interview equipment, EVIE, devised by technology boffins in the 2060s. The video changed colour if it detected the speaker was lying. This had replaced the old lie detector used in times past. Gills preferred to speak face to face as he often said, 'Makes it too easy. Any prat could be a detective using this gadget. I prefer real old-fashioned detective work.'

Gills showed his warrant card to the gatekeeper and drove up to the Hall. It was looking very grand these days because the hotel attracted a lot of guests.

The First Duke of Bartonshire had been granted the title for distinguished service to the Crown in the army, led by General James Wolfe, in the war against the old enemy, namely the French, in Canada. The newly crowned King George III had also granted the Duke twenty thousand acres in Bartonshire, and ten thousand pounds *per annum* for life, an enormous sum in those days.

Gills parked his outdated petrol-engine car, a battered-looking red Ford (*If it ain't broken, why change?* Was Gills' thought on motorcars) among the Bentleys and Rolls Royces of the paying guests. He got some snobbish looks from the owners and chauffeurs. Gills smiled inwardly. He loathed pomposity and snobbery. He ascended the grand steps to the terrace in front of the house and rapped with the huge iron doorknocker. One of the staff opened the door after a few minutes.

'Good afternoon, sir,' she said, looking askance at Gills' clothing. 'Can I be of assistance?' *Obviously not a customer,* she surmised.

He showed his warrant card and said, 'Yes, you can. I wish to speak with the Duke if he is at home?'

'Yes, sir, he has just arrived back a few minutes ago. If you would care to wait in the reception area, I shall inform him you are here, Inspector.'

Gills was shown into an ornate room with a reception desk and several carved and gilded chairs, upholstered in crimson fabric. Gills sat down and waited, flicking through some magazines. *Hmm, at least these are recent,* he chuckled to himself. *I remember finding one in the dentist's waiting room with an item about the "recent" first moon landing.*

Five minutes late the Duke, Frederick Beaumont, the Eleventh Duke, who had been Prime Minister for many years as the Member of Parliament for Bartonshire East, entered briskly even though he was in his seventies, and Gills stood. They shook hands.

'Good afternoon, Inspector. Gills, isn't it? I have seen you on television. I'm Fred Beaumont. Sorry for keeping you waiting. How may I help you?'

Gills said, 'Yes, Gills. Good afternoon, Your Grace, I am here regarding the body which was recently found buried in the cathedral.'

'Oh, just call me Fred, Inspector. Yes, I heard about that. Dreadful business. Do you suspect something sinister? I suppose there must be, or you wouldn't be here. Is there some connection with the Hall?' Fred looked puzzled.

'Just call me Gills, as in fish,' Gills said. The duke chuckled. Gills continued, 'It is suspicious, shall we say. He didn't bury himself! About the year 2040, we think.' Gills did not wish to go into details.

'Let's go into my study. We can talk there,' Fred said, and indicated with a hand gesture. Some guests were obviously trying to listen in. They walked down a short corridor to a room marked "PRIVATE". 'Would you like coffee?' Fred asked.

Gills replied, 'Yes. That would be welcome. Thank you. Been a while since breakfast. No milk or sugar, sweet enough as I am,' Gills chuckled. They sat down and Fred pressed the intercom and ordered coffee.

'Right then, how may I help you, Inspector... erm... Gills?' Fred asked. 'I'm not sure what help I may give. Surely the victim had no connection with the hotel?'

'We have a description of the young man, the deceased.' Gills then read out what the pathologist had said. 'A man in the cathedral described a similar person from the Hall, who was in the habit of visiting during choir practices back around that time. Does anything ring a bell with you, Fred?'

A secretary knocked the door and brought in a tray laden with coffee and biscuits.

'Back in 2040, you say. I would have been thirty then. I was a young MP at that time, so was away quite a bit. All very bright-eyed and bushy-tailed as they say, and out to save the nation,' Fred replied with a chuckle. 'Let me think.' He sipped his coffee, thoughtfully. 'It's a while ago. Most of the children of the original families, there were eleven families including us: my parents, my sister and myself, from London who moved here, had gone on to other things by then. Flown the nest as they say. So, who might have been here at that time?' Fred paused and again sipped his coffee. His eyes flitted from his cup to Gills and back.

'No, off-hand I cannot think of anybody who... wait a moment though. The only lad who comes to mind, who would fit that description, would have been Dwayne, Dwayne Middleton. Big strong lad he was. Would have been maybe twenty-eight or -nine then. He was just a little younger than me. He spent a lot of time in the little gym we have here as he was unemployed. Which reminds me, I must order some new equipment.' He made a note on a pad as he spoke. 'I don't know off-hand whether he liked the choir music or not. I suppose young folk would hardly broadcast the fact: it wouldn't have been *cool* as they said back then. There's probably a new word in vogue now. Most were into more modern stuff if you could call it music. I prefer jazz, myself,' Fred said. Gills smiled.

'Dwayne came back here to the Hall for a few months, or possibly a year or two, after he graduated. I can't be certain. I have no idea where he lived in between. I tell a lie: he went to London for a fleeting time job-hunting,' Fred continued. 'He went to university when he was about nineteen, studied law or something. But my memory is a bit hazy. No, it was psychology.

'Come to think of it, Dwayne did just seem to disappear quite suddenly. I came home one weekend and he had gone. It could well have been around 2040. Both his parents were dead, so we assumed he just had no reason to stay around. Sad really, because he was a nice lad, mostly. He could be quite truculent at times. Bit of a bully truth be told. Though I did wonder at the time why he never said goodbye,' he mused. 'Yes, incredibly sad.'

'Why "truculent"?' Gills asked.

'Oh, just that he had a quick temper at times. As he got older, he changed. Could have been the pressure of exams. He could be quite sharp, bullying, with the other lads. I spoke to him about it a few times. Not violent or anything, though.'

'Thank you, Fred. That is most helpful. Do you recall which university he went to?' Gills asked.

'Birmingham, I think. Yes, it was Aston, Birmingham. I remember him joking about not understanding the "Brum-mie" dialect.'

'I don't blame him. One of our detectives comes from there, and he occasionally slips into dialect.

'Right. Do you know which dentist he might have used, by any chance?' Gills asked.

'Dentist? Most of the folk went to Mr Fitzpatrick in Edward Street in the city. He's dead of course years ago and his son runs the place now. I couldn't say if Dwayne went there or not, though,' Fred said. 'Come to think of it he probably never needed one. He was always brushing his teeth. If he ate a sweet, he would go and brush. It was a sort of an ongoing joke among the folk here.'

'How did he dress? Cheap stuff or expensive?' Gills asked.

'Oh, Dwayne was always one for good clothes. Never stinted himself in that respect,' Fred replied. 'Dapper Dwayne, we called him.'

'Hmm, odd when he was unemployed, don't you think?' Gills said.

'Now you mention it, it does seem a bit odd, Inspector,' said Fred.

'Okay, thanks for your help, Fred. Goodbye,' said Gills, and they shook hands.

'Oh, before you go, perhaps I should mention he has a brother, a younger brother, Darren. He joined the Royal Air Force. Completely crazy about aircraft since he was no age. We visited RAF Barton when we came here first, and he was dead set on being a pilot. I can remember him running around pretending to be a plane and making engine noises. He will be a little younger than my age if he is still alive. Again, I have not heard of him in years, so I have no idea where he lives. Retired by now, I'm sure.'

'Yes, thank you, Fred. I will endeavour to trace him,' said Gills, jotting this down in his notebook. 'I'll see myself out.'

He returned to his car which was still receiving disapproving looks from the guests.

Chapter Four
Dwayne Middleton

'McCormick,' Gills called the officer in from the next room.

'Yes, sir,' Detective Sergeant Sidney McCormick said, as he stuck his head round the door. He was a slim, dark-haired man of thirty years, who loved his job. 'Born to it,' his family said proudly. A tall man of immaculate appearance. He believed police officers should be well dressed. A contrast to Gills in almost every respect.

'Sid, will you get onto the electoral office people, driving licences, passport office. And see if they have a record of Dwayne Middleton after 2040,' Gills said.

'Yes, I have made a start on that already, sir. Just waiting for return calls, and he has no criminal record,' said McCormick.

'Excellent! That's good work, Sid. Initiative is what I like to see. Keep it up.' Gills grinned.

McCormick was pleased. *I'll be Chief Constable soon, and be your boss,* he thought, and chuckled to himself.

Next morning, Gills called his team together.

'Are you wearing that tie for a bet, Sid?' he joked. Everyone laughed. McCormick was used to Gills' remarks and laughed too.

'Okay, has anyone anything to report on this Dwayne Middleton?' Gills asked hopefully.

'Nothing from the electoral office, Boss,' said D S McCormick. 'There are a few guys of that name, but all are too young to be our man. There was a Dwayne Middleton aged fifty-five in 2040, so, too old, who had a driving licence, but anyway he lived in Sheffield, so definitely not him. There are currently no "Dwayne Middletons" holding a passport, nor were there any in or around 2040.'

'A dead end. I was afraid of that. So, it could point to our "Corpse in the Cathedral", as the press have called him, being the local lad. We need to identify him. Any suggestions?' Gills asked.

'His dental records, sir, or DNA?' suggested D C Sally Day.

'Unfortunately, the teeth of the victim were perfect. No fillings at all. Fred Beaumont, the Duke out at Barton Hall, gave me the name of the dentist most of his folk used back then, but it seems our Dwayne never used that practice. But it seems Dwayne was fanatical about cleaning his teeth, so it could be him, or just a coincidence. His parents are dead, but he had a brother, so DNA is a possibility if we can trace him.'

'We could try round some other dentists in the city, sir,' D C Day suggested.

'Yes, you get on to that, Doris… erm…' Gills hesitated.

'Sally, sir,' she corrected, smiling.

'Ah, yes, Sally. It's just you always remind me of Doris Day.'

'Who?' Sally looked blankly at him.

'The actress, Doris Day, film "Calamity Jane", great singer too, what a voice. Lovely lass she was. She died in

2019, if I remember correctly. Before your time I suppose. Before my time too, actually,' Gills explained, 'but I love old films.

'Anyway, see what you can find. Hopefully, a twenty-something lad with perfect gnashers,' Gills commented.

There were some chuckles from the crew.

Chapter Five
Darren Middleton

Having drawn a blank, so far, trying to trace Dwayne's present whereabouts, if still alive, Gills decided to try his brother Darren for DNA. He telephoned the Royal Air Force pensions department to see if Darren Middleton was still receiving a pension.

'Yes, Inspector,' a clerk replied, 'he is still receiving a service pension and war injuries allowance.'

'Can I have his address, please?' Gills asked. The clerk gave him the address and Gills grabbed his coat calling Sid to follow and set off for Darren Middleton's address in Oxford. 'Just as well he is not in South America or someplace,' he muttered.

'I wouldn't mind going to South America, sir,' Sid said, with a grin. Gills shook his head as if to say, *No chance*.

Darren answered the door. He was on crutches with a leg amputated at the knee. He had a prosthetic limb but rarely wore it at home as it was uncomfortable at times. 'What do you want?' he asked gruffly.

'I am Detective Inspector Gills, and this is Detective Sergeant McCormick of the Bartonshire Constabulary. Are you

Darren Middleton formerly of Barton Hall?' Gills asked, showing his warrant card.

'That I am. What's this about, Detective Inspector?'

'May we come in, sir?' replied Gills.

'Well, I suppose so. I'm not going anywhere.' Smiling wryly, he indicated his lack of a right leg.

When they were seated Gills asked, 'Mr Middleton, I am trying to trace your brother Dwayne. When did you last see him?'

Darren hesitated for a few seconds in surprise and then asked, 'Our Dwayne? Why do you want him? What's he supposed to have done?'

'He hasn't done anything. I just need to speak to him to eliminate him from an inquiry.'

'Well, I haven't seen my brother in years, Inspector,' Darren replied looking uneasy.

'You may have read that a body was recently discovered buried in Market Barton Cathedral. I need to be sure it was not him.'

'You... you think it was Dwayne... our Dwayne... in the cathedral?' Darren exclaimed looking shocked. 'I read about it, but Dwayne!? It couldn't be, could it?'

'Why do you say it couldn't be?' Gills asked.

'It... it's just... something you say, isn't it? You never think that bodies found could be someone you knew.'

'I'm sorry for having to tell you,' said Gills, 'but there is a strong possibility it is him.'

'That's horrible. It is just a bit of a shock to hear it could be him. I never associated the murdered man, hit over the head... probably, and buried in the cathedral, with anyone I knew, least of all my brother. You see, Inspector, I have neither seen nor heard of Dwayne since, let me think, it must be forty years ago,' Darren replied. 'Oh! That is about the time that man died, according to the papers!'

'What makes you think he was murdered?' Gills asked.

'I just assumed so because he was buried in the cathedral. The papers said so: "*Suspicious circumstances*",' Darren said. 'He did not bury himself!'

'Forty years ago, since you saw him! That's a long time ago. Why is that?' asked Gills.

'This is what happened, Inspector. He came to me, just after he graduated from Uni. Must have been in 2035 or so. He wanted money, to put it bluntly, Inspector. He said he owed a lot to some drug dealer. His eyes were kind of wild looking. He was restless, couldn't sit still.'

'Oh, how much are we talking about?' asked Gill.

'Seven thousand pounds. Quite a lot in those days. It would hardly buy a packet of cigarettes these days,' he smiled slightly. 'Not that I smoke, of course. Disgusting habit. They should have been banned years ago. Those vapour things are nearly as bad, in my opinion, but I digress. I thought it was odd, the drugs, because Dwayne was always into fitness: six-pack abs and that sort of thing. Bit of a *poseur* in fact. I had never known him to take as much as an aspirin. He was very particular about his appearance.'

'Did you mention this to him?' Gills enquired.

'Yes, of course, as I recall. He said that he had taken stuff, he didn't say what, to get through his exams. He still looked perfectly fit, so I tried to find out if there was another explanation, but he insisted it was drugs. "A matter of life and death," he said, as the dealer was "dangerous" he said. I told him I did not have that amount of money. I had just joined up, the RAF, and pay was not huge. That is how I lost my leg, an aircraft crash, shot down, in the war in the Indian Ocean back in 2051.' He pointed to the missing appendage. 'So, I gave him what I could, and he left. Never saw him again. I tried phoning and went to his last address in London that I knew of when he left university, but he was gone. I suppose I should have asked him if he was still living there, but it never occurred to me when he was with me. I lived in a small village, mostly RAF families, near the RAF Barton airbase at the time.

'I waited to hear from him, and as there were no reports in the papers of a death or such, I assumed he had managed to pay off whoever it was. I did report him missing but nothing came of it.'

'Okay. While we are here, can we take a DNA sample… just for elimination purposes?' Gills said.

'Yes, of course,' Darren replied. 'I hope it helps… proves the body isn't him, I mean.'

Sid McCormick produced a swab and a sterile vial and took a saliva sample.

'Right, that is all we need. If this confirms the body is someone else, or if we trace him, your brother, I shall let you know. Goodbye.' They shook hands and Gills and McCormick left.

Darren looked worried.

Chapter Six
A Cold Case

A few days later, Gills convened the CID detectives involved in the case.

'Right then, people, I have here the results of the DNA test on the victim.' He waved a sheet of paper. 'It seems that Dwayne Middleton is indeed the body in the cathedral. There is no doubt at all. His brother's DNA is a match.'

Murmurs of acknowledgement from the officers.

'What we need to find now is why he was murdered, and especially, by whom? We are starting from scratch as this is what might be described as a very cold case.' A few smiles at Gills' little joke.

'Has anyone any ideas on how we could proceed?' Gills asked. 'I'm open to suggestions.'

'Sir, the brother said Dwayne was in debt to a drug dealer. Must be a good reason for murder!' suggested Detective Sergeant McCormick.

'Yes, Sid. For the benefit of you other guys, the brother Darren said he came wanting to borrow a lot of cash, then he never heard from him again. He reported Dwayne missing at the time, but no trace was found…' Gills began.

'Because he was under the floorboards, presumably,' said McCormick with a grimace.

'Yes, that's probably why, Sid. We'll make a detective of you yet.' Gills gave a smile. Everyone chuckled and McCormick made a face and laughed.

'I checked our records and there was a missing-person search done, back then, but it came to nothing,' said another detective.

'Hmm, okay. Now, how do we find a drug-dealer forty-something years later?' Gills asked, more to himself than to the others.

'Going to be nearly impossible. He could be dead too,' Sid McCormick murmured.

'I'll call with the brother, the only relative, myself to let him know the sad news, before the media broadcast it,' said Gills. 'It will be a shock.'

Gills went to see Darren later that day.

'Ah, it's you, Inspector. Have you any news of my brother?' Darren asked, looking anxious.

'Yes, Mr Middleton, but I'm afraid it is not good.'

Darren seemed a bit unsteady and sat down on a settee, putting his crutches to one side. 'It really was him then, the body that was found?' he asked.

'Yes, the DNA was conclusive. I'm really sorry,' Gills said with sincerity.

'It's okay, I was sort of expecting bad news. It would explain a lot, but of course, I was just hoping…'

'Of course. Now, we need to find his killer, or killers. Can you recall anything else Dwayne said that day? I know it is a long time ago, but anything that might give us a lead,' said Gills.

Darren thought for a moment. 'Been going over it in my head since you were last here. As far as I can remember, he said: "I need to borrow some cash. A lot of cash." I asked why, and he said: "I have got into debt with a drug dealer." He said definitely "a dealer" singular. Then: "I needed something to get me through my final exams, but then I was hooked on the stuff." He didn't say what, but I assumed some mind booster or such. I asked how much he owed, and I think he said seven thousand pounds, as I told you earlier. I said I did not have that kind of cash, so I got as much as I could scrape together, about two thousand. I told him if I could scrape together some more I would do so. He was scared-looking, but he said I had been a good help and there was nothing more I could do, that he needed the rest in a hurry, and he left. The rest you know, Inspector.'

'Thank you, Mr Middleton. And I am sorry for having to bring this news,' said Gills.

'I appreciate you coming, Inspector. At least now we can give him a proper Christian burial. "Ashes to ashes, dust to dust" as they say. Thank you,' Darren replied.

'I will let you know when the remains are released for burial,' Gills said and then left. When back in his car he pondered on what Darren had said. *Not a lot to go on,* he thought. *I just hope forensics can come up with something, for it's fairly pointless looking for a drug-dealer after all this time, who might even be dead, too, as Sid said.*

Next day, in the forensic laboratory, Gills asked if anything new had been discovered.

'Yes, indeed, Inspector,' said the technician, Olwyn Williams who had a strong Welsh accent. 'There is absolutely no residue of drugs in the hair samples, so presumably he had stopped using for some years. Some hair was preserved, probably due to the dry soil, but we did find this, Inspector.' She held up a badly corroded metal button. 'This was clutched in the deceased bloke's right hand... brass or some yellow metal, looks like. We did not notice it straight away because there was soil caked between the finger bones. I assume when the victim fell dying, and before he was wrapped in plastic. We lifted the surrounding soil as usual. Chances are it belonged to the murderer. The victim probably grabbed the murderer's jacket and tore it off. He or she may not have noticed it missing until after the body was buried.'

'Hmm, interesting. And no drugs,' Gills murmured as he held up the button and examined it. 'It was most likely a man, the killer, as he would have needed to be pretty strong to have hauled Dwayne around. He was a big guy by all accounts.'

'Yes, I would say so, maybe 100 kilos at least,' said the technician, 'going by his bones.'

Chapter Seven
The Duke

'Thank you for seeing me again, Duke… erm… Fred,' said Gills as he once more sat in Fred's study in the Hall.

'Not a problem, Inspector,' Fred replied. 'What's up? I'll help in any way I can.'

'It's the body in the cathedral, or skeleton. I'm sure you have heard it is definitely that of Dwayne Middleton.'

'Yes, Market Barton is a small place when it comes to news,' Fred replied. 'The grapevine could compete with the BBC. Such a sad end.'

'Did you ever see the brother Darren here, around the time Dwayne disappeared?'

'Surely you don't…?' Fred looked shocked.

'I am just building some background for the moment, Fred. Darren may have been one of the last to see his brother alive,' said Gills. 'He said he last saw him in 2035, or thereabouts.'

'Well, as I recall, that was about when Dwayne finished university.' Fred delved in a desk drawer. 'I found this photo of him at his graduation. I remembered he went to London for a short time looking for a job, but he returned and was living here at the Hall for maybe four or five years after that.

'I have been thinking about it since your last visit, and I am pretty certain of that. I cannot be precise, but I'm sure he was still around in 2040. The young ones were always coming and going back then.'

Gills looked at the photo and said, 'So, he was living here from university, more or less?'

'He went to London for a few weeks, I think. He was hoping for a London job, as I said, but he came back here definitely. That would have been when the choristers saw him in the cathedral. He became a bit withdrawn as I recall. I spoke to him once, but he just shrugged his shoulders and said he was okay,' Fred said. 'He got angry when I mentioned it a few days later and we had a bit of a falling out. I'm afraid things were a bit tense after that. I don't know what was on his mind.'

'And Darren?'

'Yes, Darren visited a few times… up until Dwayne disappeared, I'm sure. It's so long ago. Then I don't recall seeing him again either. He was in the RAF by then. I supposed he was serving abroad. I didn't think much about him to be honest.'

'He was wounded in the Indian Ocean War.'

'Oh, that was much later, in the 2050s. There was a write-up in the local paper at the time. Leg or arm amputated if I remember correctly. He got a medal for bravery: saved the lives of his crew.'

'Yes, a leg. So, he disappeared too, more or less,' said Gills.

'Yes, I suppose so. He had no ties with the Hall. With his brother gone and his parents dead, there were no ties,' said Fred.

'Yes, quite so. Did they ever argue, Dwayne and Darren?' Gills asked.

'Let me think. Yes, a couple of times, I was passing Dwayne's room at the back of the building, and I heard raised voices. Couldn't make out what was being said but it was definitely heated. But then siblings do argue on occasion. My daughters were always squabbling. They still do.' Fred smiled.

'And it was Darren who was there?' asked Gills.

'Yes, Darren slept in Dwayne's room when he visited. It is a large room. Most of the rooms here are large.'

'Yes, I have noticed. Who uses it now?' Gills asked.

'Oh, let me think. Yes, a Miss Polly. She's a lady chef. "Polly, put the kettle on" is a favourite joke by the staff in the kitchen. She often stays over when there is a late banquet, or an early shift as she lives quite a distance away and hates driving a night. Some guests wish to leave early to catch planes *et cetera*. She uses the room for free as we don't require it for guests.'

'Did you have to remove Dwayne's things from the room?' Gills asked.

'Yes, now you mention it. It's all coming back to me. Getting old I'm afraid, memory's not what it used to be. Well, when he was not heard of for some months, his stuff, not that there was a lot, was stored in a box in an attic. Do you wish to see it? I suppose it is still there, Inspector,' Fred said.

'Yes. I'll get a detective to collect it later. Forensics, you know,' Gills said.

'Oh, yes, there may be some clues,' said Fred. 'Though there was only the usual personal stuff: clothes and toiletries, electric shaver, as I recall. Stuff you would normally take with you if you were moving. But it seems poor Dwayne never got the chance. Oh, and there was some cash… about five hundred pounds if I remember correctly. I put it in the hotel safe for him returning. I'll get it now. Give me a minute.' Fred went to the safe, entered the security code and hoked around. 'Ah, here it is at the back!' He handed an envelope to Gills. 'I had quite forgotten about it.'

'A lot of cash for an unemployed man,' Gills murmured.

'Yes, indeed,' said Fred.

'By the way, were you living here at the time or in London?' Gills asked. 'The problem is, there was a missing person search done when Darren reported him missing. Why were the clothes and money not mentioned to the police at the time?'

'You don't suspect…?'

'Just a routine question, Fred,' Gills replied.

'Well, parliament was in recess at the time, spring break. I was living here and doing a bit of constituency work,' Fred said. 'Plus, it was nice to spend some time with my parents.' He paused. 'I can only surmise that the police called while I was in my constituency office. My staff must have told them he had just left without a trace. They wouldn't have known of the clothes and money.'

'I see. Thank you, Fred. I'll see myself out,' Gills said, and they shook hands.

Later, in the forensic science laboratory, Gills and McCormick were looking through all that Dwayne had left behind.

'Some old clothes, Inspector,' said the lab assistant. 'Nothing in the pockets except the money you got. Some toiletries… and this.' Gills was handed something interesting.

Gills flicked through a small notebook and turned towards his detective sergeant. 'Take a look at that, Sid.'

Sid read out a list of numbers on the final page used: '725, 350, 400, 500.'

Gills said, 'There were five hundred pounds in his pocket! Which he never had the opportunity to dispose of. I have the feeling there was something not *kosher* going on. I've had an idea. Send a car, Sid, and get the brother lifted and in here for an interview. And tell him to call his lawyer,' Gills shouted at McCormick's retreating back.

Chapter Eight
An Arrest

Later in an inquiry room, D S McCormick said, 'Darren Middleton, I arrest you on suspicion of the murder of Dwayne Middleton. You do not have to say anything, but it may harm your defence if you do not mention something, when questioned, you later rely on in court.' Darren's mouth dropped open.

'Why has my client been arrested, Inspector? On what evidence?' the lawyer asked.

'Because he has committed a crime, Mr Boston,' Gills said flatly, and turned to Darren.

Gills spoke, 'An interview recorded today, the twentieth day of April 2084. Those present: Mr Darren Middleton, his lawyer Mr James Boston, Detective Inspector Irvine Gills, and Detective Sergeant Sidney McCormick.

'Mr Middleton, I would like to ask you a few questions,' Gills said. Darren nodded but said nothing.

'You stated some weeks ago that you last saw your brother,' Gills consulted his notebook, 'you said, in 2035: "Must have been in 2035 or so." Is that correct?'

'Yeah, that's right. I'm sure it was in 2035,' replied Darren.

'I have information that you visited your brother, at Barton Hall, right up until he disappeared in 2040, Mr Middleton,' Gills said, forcefully.

'Erm, maybe I did. It's ages ago. How am I supposed to remember that far back?' Darren protested. 'I had just joined up and what with training and flying here, there and yonder, it is all a blur really. Of course, it was before I lost my leg,' Darren asserted.

'You said that Dwayne came to you looking for money to pay a drug-dealer. Is that correct?'

'Yeah, I told you all this,' Darren replied.

'I must inform you that forensics found no trace of drugs in your brother's remains. None, at all, not even of an aspirin, Mr Middleton.'

Darren looked at his lawyer then back at Gills. 'He said it was drugs. Erm… there must be some mistake.'

'No mistake.' Gills then placed the small book, in a plastic evidence bag, on the table in front of Darren.

Darren stared at it, and he thought what it might be. He looked perturbed.

'This, Mr Middleton, is your late brother's notebook, a sort of diary, wherein he wrote several things. Do you think he may have recorded the dates and the amounts of cash he obtained from you? For example, might he have written something like "Got cash from my dear brother. What a mug! I intend to drain him dry. I'm sure the air force bigwigs would love to hear his guilty secret!!"? So, Mr Middleton, just what was your guilty secret?' Gills asked.

'I… I don't know what he meant. It's nonsense. It's just gibberish,' Darren said and looked flustered.

'On the contrary, it is perfectly clear. It appears he discovered you were taking drugs. I expect he found something when you shared a room at the Hall. Forensic officers have found minute traces of cocaine in the drawers of the furniture in that room, when we sent in the sniffer dogs, Mr Middleton. The present occupant, a middle-aged lady, was horrified. Obviously, Dwayne was not the user.'

'It must have been someone else, Detective Inspector.' Darren leaned on the table and angrily began to stand. His lawyer restrained his arm as McCormick took a step forward. 'I have never taken drugs. I was a pilot, for goodness' sake. A jet pilot. I would have been out on my ear for taking drugs.'

'I now wish you to identify this button, if you will, which was found clenched in the soil under the hand bones of the deceased.' Gills showed him a button in a plastic evidence bag. 'It is an RAF button, albeit badly corroded, from the sleeve of a uniform. The local RAF Commanding Officer has verified this. Was it off your uniform? I suspect you discovered it missing, but the flooring of the transept had already been replaced when you returned. Am I on the right track?' Gills asked. 'You were certain it would be centuries before the body was found.' Darren was too shaken to reply.

'Your career would have been *kaput,* if the authorities knew that you, a pilot, were on drugs, would it not, Mr Middleton?' Gills asked.

'I have never taken drugs, Detective. Never! I was reluctant to even take morphine when I lost my leg.'

'By the way, how did you know the deceased...' Gills consulted his notes, '... had been, I quote, "hit over the head and buried in the cathedral", unquote? There was no mention in the media of the means of death.'

Darren looked like he was going to be sick. 'I… I just assumed he was struck with something. Could not have been shot for it would have been like thunder in that building. A knife, I suppose, but being hit just came into my head. It always says on the TV "the deceased was struck with a blunt instrument" doesn't it?'

'Why were you and your brother often heard arguing in your room at the Hall?'

'We were always arguing about something. Dwayne was as stubborn as a mule. He would never see sense about anything,' Darren replied.

'Can you explain how the traces of cocaine found in the room you shared got there, Mr Middleton?' Gills asked.

Darren hesitated for a few moments, then said, 'That was one of the things we argued about. I found him one day filling little plastic bags with a drug. I demanded to know what he was up to. He just laughed, like he always did and shouted that it was none of my business. I left the Hall for good after that. I stayed on the airbase.'

'Just one thing puzzles me, Mr Middleton: why bury him in the cathedral?' asked Gills.

Darren sat with his head in his hands for some minutes. The others waited patiently. Gills let him stew. He looked at his watch… straighten his bowtie… looked at his watch again.

Finally, Darren spoke. 'Okay, I shall tell all I know. This is the truth. I'm not covering for him any longer. I did not want the shame on the family of anyone knowing that my brother was a dealer.

'He did not come to me for money, he had been forcing me to bank money for him in my account for about four or

204

five years. He was unemployed but still had a lot of money. It was not difficult to figure where he got it… dealing drugs!

'He was an unemployed bully. Ever since he escaped from a fire at the Hall when we were young, he became so full of himself and he bullied all the kids, the lads anyway. He thought all the girls were crazy about him. They weren't.

'Then he decided to force me to stash the money for him. Those amounts in that notebook are what he gave me each week or so. He did not want large sums lying around his room in the Hall, so he visited me or met me in a pub. I noticed he had the amounts written down. He obviously did not trust me. He had quite a hefty sum stashed.'

'Where is the money now?' Gills asked.

'After he disappeared, I did not want it sitting in my bank account, so I withdrew it and put it in a different bank, the Bartonshire Savings Bank. It is still there. I wanted nothing to do with it.

'He said he would tell my CO, Commanding Officer, I was a junkie if I did not cooperate. That is what our rows in the room were about. He would not see reason.'

'So, you killed him?' McCormick asked.

'No, never. I just couldn't keep doing it any longer, so late one evening, when I had just arrived in the city from the RAF base, I saw him going into the cathedral as he was fond of the music, incongruous as that may seem. I followed him on an impulse. The choir practice had been cancelled for some reason, or had just finished, as I recall. Anyway, the place was deserted. The only lights were in the chancel. The nave was in darkness.

'He was looking through the plastic dust sheet into the part where the repair work was being done. I went up to him and asked him, I begged him, to stop demanding I hide his money, but he just laughed in my face. "You must be joking. I need your account, and there is nothing you can do about it, dear brother. If you don't cooperate, I will tell your boss you are a drug user," he said. Dwayne was not the nice guy people thought he was. I have never taken drugs. Four years I put up with him, and finally, I could take no more. I was afraid I would be an accessory if he were caught drug dealing. That would have ended my career for sure. I saw red and punched him on the jaw. I just lost it, Inspector. I thought my hand was broken for days after. He fell on his backside and sat nursing his jaw. I thought, I hoped, I had broken it to teach him a lesson. He was alive when I left. Very much alive. He shouted he would get even. I just kept walking and I never saw him again. I assumed he had learnt his lesson when I never heard from him again, though I did wonder why he didn't come for his stash of loot.

'I never noticed the button missing until later, as you said. He must have grabbed my sleeve as he fell back. But when I returned the next day, the workmen had started to replace the floor, and I could see no sign of it, so I just left.

'I went overseas a few days later, with a posting to the Middle East, and eventually took part in the war in the Indian Ocean. Fighting over some tiny islands. I returned to England after I was injured, left the base and moved to Oxford… and that's about it,' Darren finished.

'Sergeant, take him out,' Gills ordered. 'I will give you police bail while I check your story, Middleton.'

When McCormick returned, the lawyer having left, he said to Gills, 'Sir, I was sure we had our man. It is difficult, though, to believe he would have murdered his own brother.

206

He must be telling the truth. Maybe we should have used the video screen to check he wasn't lying?'

'Fratricide is more common than people would think,' Gills replied. 'That's what the crime statistics show. Speaking personally, this is the third case I have encountered in my long and illustrious career.' Gills raised an eyebrow and smiled at McCormick grinned. 'First case was just after I became a detective. Younger sister fancied her sibling's boyfriend, and he fancied her as it turned out, and they hatched the murder plot.

'The second was, let me think, a year or two later. Younger brother wanted the title and inheritance due to his older brother. The Earl of somewhere or other. Lots of land, big house. Anyway, little brother pushed the heir off a cliff up in the Scottish Highlands. Only snag was a birdwatcher a mile away was filming a lesser-spotted finch or a bird of some kind. Anyway with a telephoto lens or something. Caught it all on camera! Poor man nearly had a heart attack. Upshot was the easiest case I ever had.

'We will check out Darren's version tomorrow, Sid. As you say, he may be telling the truth.'

'Here, sir, what was all that diary stuff?' asked D S McCormick, 'It was only some numbers, wasn't it, not what you said?'

'That, Sid, was what is called in the trade, a bluff.' Gills grinned broadly. 'I did say "might he have written", didn't I? Darren knew that because Dwayne was giving him money, not *vice versa*. Tomorrow we start checking who else may have wanted Dwayne dead, though it is over forty years ago.

Chapter Nine
A Hairline Fracture

At nine-thirty, next morning, Gills and McCormick were with Mr Stuart in the mortuary.

Stuart said, 'Okay, Irvine, what's up?'

'Our suspect in the Middleton case, says he punched him, Dwayne, on the chin, hard. Can you verify that in any way from the jawbone?' Gills replied.

'Hmm, let's take a look.' Stuart bent over with a magnifying glass and examined the bone.

'Yep, there is a fine hairline fracture I never noticed before. This guy would not have made a boxer. His jawbone would not have been up to it. The fracture was made just prior to death as it had not started to repair itself. So, quite possibly, as your suspect said, but of course he could then have gone on the clobber him with that candlestick. One matched the injury, by the way.'

'Or someone else could have clobbered him when the suspect had left,' McCormick offered.

'Good point, problem is, who?' said Gills. 'Right, thanks, Jack. Thanks for your help.'

The three men shook hands.

Back at the car Gills said, 'We will head back to the Hall. We need to find out who else Dwayne was bullying. Maybe someone was pushed to their limit. Okay, let's go.' He tossed the car keys to McCormick.

McCormick was the only person whom Gills allowed to drive his car.

'Ah, good morning, Inspector, and you…?' Fred welcomed them at the door, and they proceeded to his office.

'This is Detective Sergeant Sidney McCormick, Fred. He is my right-hand man,' Gills introduced Sid.

'Welcome to you too, Sergeant. Are you married? We are presently doing a very reasonably priced wedding reception package,' Fred said jokingly.

'Erm, I am as it happens,' McCormick replied grinning. 'Very happily as a matter of fact.'

'Which means he does what he's told,' Gills joked.

'No matter. How may I help? I thought you had your suspect?' Fred asked.

'Well, there are a few snags. Mainly, he didn't do it, as far as we can ascertain,' said Gills.

'Oh, obviously someone did. Any other suspects in the frame?' Fred asked.

'We need to ask you a few more questions about Dwayne Middleton,' Gills replied.

'Okay, fire away. I don't know if there is much more I can tell you,' said Fred.

'We have received information that Dwayne was bullying some other lads here at the Hall, forcing them, possibly, to some illegal activity. Does anyone else come to mind?'

'Give me a minute to think who would still have been living here in 2040. The young ones were coming and going all the time,' Fred said. 'There was Tommy Jameson junior, James Wu, and possibly Johnny Higginson. They were all about the same age as Dwayne and me.'

'Did he ever approach you about anything illegal?' Gills asked.

'No, he certainly did not. He would have known I would have gone straight to the police.'

'Are those three men still alive?' McCormick asked.

'Yes, they are. All old like me now though,' Fred chuckled. 'James still lives at the Hall, and I could give you the addresses of the others. Johnny is a widower, and his sister Kate lives with him since her husband died a few years ago. I can't recall his name.'

'That's good. Thank you, Fred. Is James here at the moment?' Gills asked.

Fred checked the time with a wall-clock. 'No, he will be at the restaurant in the city, "The Golden Dragon".'

'Okay, thanks again,' Gills said, and they left.

Chapter Ten
The Golden Dragon

The two detectives went to the restaurant in the city and asked to see Mr Wu.

'Ah, I'm James Wu, how may I help you?' James said as he wiped his hands on an apron.

'I'm Detective Inspector Gills and this is Detective Sergeant McCormick. We would like to speak to you about the late Dwayne Middleton, Mr Wu.'

'Yeah, I heard he was murdered. Not missed very much as far as I am concerned,' James replied.

'You and he were not best mates then?' Gills asked.

'That's putting it mildly, Inspector. But I did not kill him before you ask. He turned into one of the nastiest, hateful blokes I have ever known,' James said.

'Why was that?' Gills asked.

'Well, to put it bluntly, he was a small-time drug dealer and because I refused to launder his money through the restaurant, he made my life a misery. A bully he was from his teens. I don't mind saying I was relieved when he left, as I thought then. Seems he did not leave after all.'

'You knew he was dealing, so why not report it to the police?' Gills asked.

'I suppose I should have, but I was thinking he would be caught sooner or later. And if I had reported him and he got off, he would have sought revenge. I sort of thought he had cleared out because the cops were suspicious. Not that I gave him much thought. Like I said, he was a nasty person,' James said.

'Well, thank you, Mr Wu. We may have to question you again. Don't leave the country as they say,' said Gills.

'I have nothing to hide, and I certainly have no intention of going anywhere, Inspector. Now, if I may get back to work?' James said. 'I am wasting no more time over Middleton.'

'Yes, and thanks for your time,' Gills replied. The two officers left and returned to their car.

They next went to the address of Tommy Jameson Jnr. He lived in the suburbs of Market Barton in a detached house with well-kept gardens.

Gills produced his warrant card and introduced themselves when Mrs Jameson, an attractive elderly lady, opened the door.

'May we speak to your husband if he is at home, Mrs Jameson? I assume you are his wife,' said Gills.

'Yes, I am indeed. He is in the garden at the back. His tomatoes, you know; fanatical about them.' she laughed. 'If you would care to wait in the lounge, I shall call him,' she said.

The two officers sat in expensive leather armchairs in a rather tastefully decorated large room, with a small grand piano in one corner and several bookshelves and other furniture around the room.

'Done well for himself has Mr Jameson by the looks of things,' Sid McCormick commented.

'Yes, not short of a few quid for sure,' said Gills.

A few minutes later, the Jamesons returned. He was in his socks having removed his "gardening boots" as he called them. Mrs Jameson did not permit these to enter the house. 'I'm not cleaning floors for you to traipse in with muddy boots,' she said frequently.

'Ah, Inspector, how may I be of assistance?' Tommy asked. He was a distinguished-looking elderly man with grey hair and moustache. He and his wife took a sofa opposite the officers.

'I am sure you have heard of the death of Dwayne Middleton, Mr Jameson. Do you recall when you last saw him?' Gills asked.

'Oh, that was a long time ago. Let me think. It would have been about a year before he disappeared. We now know why. I assume it was murder? Someone obviously caught up with him,' Tommy smiled slightly. Gills just nodded. McCormick was taking notes.

'I had just qualified as a psychiatrist and was still living at the Hall. I suppose you have been there?' Tommy paused. Gills nodded that he had. 'Well, long story short, I moved out because I was not prepared to put up with Dwayne's bullying any longer. I got a mortgage for this house, met my beautiful wife Emily, and have been here since.' Mrs Jameson smiled lovingly at her husband.

'In what way was Dwayne a bully?' Gills asked.

'You name it, and he did it, Inspector. Generally making everyone's life miserable. Belittling all we did, sniping remarks about people's appearance. I was rather flabby in those

213

days, and he continually commented on it at every opportunity especially when we went swimming in the lake. Really nasty, snide remarks, not just banter likes kids do.

'The last straw was when he tried to sell me his drugs. In my position, I dared not even consider taking drugs, but Dwayne was constantly at me to try them. "Go on, give them a try. They'll do you good," he would say. Yes, I know I should have reported him, but it was difficult with a guy I had grown up with since we were... well, all our lives really, in London and in the Hall.' His wife patted his arm comfortingly.

'I understand, Mr Jameson. Anyway, it is in the past now,' Gills said. 'Had you any contact with him after you moved here?'

'Not really. He did appear at my door once, as I recall, but I told him to clear off and threatened to set the dog on him. I had a German shepherd back then. Big soft thing he was but Dwayne didn't know that. And a while later, I heard he had gone. For good, I hoped. Now we know why: dumped off in the cathedral of all places.

'No, few will mourn Dwayne Middleton, Inspector. Sorry if that sounds harsh but he was a horrible man.'

'Okay, thank you for your time, Mr Jameson, and you too Mrs Jameson. If we need to speak to you again, I shall be in touch,' Gills said.

Back in the car, McCormick commented, 'Nobody liked this guy did they, Boss?'

'They certainly did not, Sid. But that does not mean they killed him. Not enough motive. People don't kill everyone they dislike, thankfully. Let's try that last guy. What's his name?'

Sid looked at his notebook, 'Mr Johnny Higginson, Boss.'

'Look at the time!' Gills consulted his watch. 'Okay, let's have lunch and chase him up later. I'm famished,' Gills chuckled.

'We should have eaten at Mr Wu's,' said McCormick. He licked his lips.

'Could be construed as a conflict of interest,' Gills chuckled.

Chapter Eleven
Johnny and Kate

'Mr John Higginson?' Gills asked.

'Yep, that's me,' Johnny Higginson replied at his front door.

'I am Detective Inspector Gills, and this is Detective Sergeant McCormick of the Bartonshire Constabulary. May we come in?'

'Yeah sure.' Higginson stepped aside and indicated the living room. The two officers entered and sat down after shaking hands.

'I suppose this is about Middleton. I heard his body has been found in the cathedral,' Higginson said.

'Yes, Mr Higginson, we are investigating his murder. When did you last see him?' asked Gills.

'Oh, many years ago, Inspector…' An elderly lady came into the room.

'What's going on, John?' she asked. 'Who are these men?'

'Two policemen investigating the death of Dwayne Middleton, Kate.' She went pale and sat down clasping her hands on her lap. 'Inspector, this is my sister Kate Best. She is a widow and moved here when my own wife died some years ago,' Higginson said.

Gills shook hands, 'I am sorry to have to do this, Mrs Best, but we must investigate the death. We are interviewing folk who knew him at the Hall,' Gills said.

'I understand. It is just a shock to hear his name after all these years. Dreadful man he was,' Kate Best replied.

'Dwayne, as I am sure you know, was murdered. When did you last see him?'

'As I was saying, Inspector, it was many years ago. I left the Hall in 2039. To be frank, it was Dwayne who drove me away. I shouldn't speak ill of the dead, but he was an awful person,' Higginson said.

'Why was that, Mr Higginson?'

'No harm in telling all now I suppose...' Higginson began. Mrs Best seemed about to stop him. 'Don't worry, Kate, it is better they hear the truth. Inspector, Dwayne was a drug dealer. He got me hooked on stuff and I got into debt as I was an addict before long. I went into rehab later and got off it, for a while, but he hounded me for money. Nasty, vicious man he was. Started beating me up when I had no cash yet kept giving me more drugs. I was a hopeless case. Kate took me away to live with her and Mr Best, Oliver Best, until I was rehabilitated. Then I met my wife June, and we got this little house, and I left the Hall.

'Dwayne suddenly disappeared, and we breathed a sigh of relief. We assumed some gang had done him in.'

'Had we not got John away from the Hall he would be dead, Inspector. Dwayne Middleton was an evil man,' Mrs Best added.

'I understand,' said Gills. 'So, you never saw him since you left the Hall, Mr Higginson?'

'Oh, he kept after me until Kate and Oliver paid him off: the money I owed him. Then he quit and we heard he had gone from the Hall. No one knew, or cared, what happened to him, to be honest,' Higginson said. 'I'm glad somebody knocked his head in…' Higginson hesitated. Mrs Best gasped.

'Why do you use that expression, Mr Higginson?' Gills asked abruptly. D S McCormick's pencil poised over his notebook.

'Oh, erm, no reason. I… I just assumed that is what happened. Didn't it say so in the paper?'

'No, it did not. Just what do you know about his death?' Gills asked loudly. Mrs Best jumped in fright.

'Nothing, nothing. It is only an expression,' Higginson cried.

'John Higginson, I arrest you on suspicion of the murder…' McCormick began to say.

'No, no! Stop! You have it all wrong! All wrong, Inspector.' Kate Best cried out throwing her arms around her brother. 'It wasn't John… it was me. I… killed… him.' Higginson tried to stop her from speaking. 'No, John, after all these years, I cannot hide it anymore.

'Inspector, this is what happened: I saw Darren, in his uniform, going into the cathedral one evening. I guessed Dwayne would be there too. I crept into the back of the nave which was unlit and crouched down in a pew. I don't know what I was intending to do. It was an impulse. Maybe I hoped Darren, he's a decent man, would speak to his brother and stop him hounding John. They were arguing up where they were doing repairs. I could not make out what they were saying, just the occasional word, and then Darren punched Dwayne on the chin. Dwayne fell back and Darren walked away.

'Dwayne was sort of groggy and was facing away from me rubbing his chin, so I ran quietly up and grabbed one of the candlesticks and hit him on the back of the head. I don't know what came over me. I'm not violent normally, but I just saw a chance to rid ourselves of him forever. Dwayne fell forward on the floor. I tried to move him, but he was too heavy, so I phoned my husband on the mobile phone and he came and helped me bury the body. Fortunately, none of the clergy were around.

'When we got home, we got cleaned up and the next day, we told John we had paid Dwayne what he was owed. John knew nothing until tonight. I am the one you want, Inspector.'

Higginson was stunned. He sat as if frozen, then he clasped his sister's hands. 'This is all my fault. If only I had not got hooked on drugs…'

'Kate Best, I arrest you on suspicion of the murder of Dwayne Middleton. You do not have to say anything, but it may harm your defence if you do not mention something, when questioned, you later rely on in court,' McCormick said and escorted her out to the car.

'Well, I would say that was my easiest case,' said Gills.

'Our easiest case, Boss,' McCormick said with a laugh.

'Okay, our easiest case. I think we earned a drink as it is your turn to pay young Sidney,' Gills said.

'Why is it always my turn to pay, Boss?'

'Okay then, we shall toss for it.' He produced a fifty pence coin. 'Heads I win, tails you lose.'

McCormick nodded then said, 'Oh no, you cannot catch me with that old joke, Boss.'

'Worth a try, Sidney. Anyway, you are still paying. Get your wallet out,' Gills laughed.

'I still think you should pay sometimes, Boss.'

'Privilege of rank, my son, privilege of rank. "Lead on Macduff".'

Sid McCormick shrugged, resigned to his fate. *Not a bad boss though, I suppose. Could be worse. Could be D I Grimly,* he thought, and laughed to himself.

The End